MW00528002

THE MORE
THE TERRIER

ALSO BY DAVID ROSENFELT

ANDY CARPENTER NOVELS

Dog Day Afternoon
'Twas the Bite Before Christmas
Flop Dead Gorgeous
Santa's Little Yelpers
Holy Chow
Best in Snow
Dog Eat Dog
Silent Bite
Muzzled
Dachshund Through the Snow
Bark of Night
Deck the Hounds
Rescued
Collared
The Twelve Dogs of Christmas
Outfoxed
Who Let the Dog Out?
Hounded
Unleashed
Leader of the Pack
One Dog Night
Dog Tags
New Tricks
Play Dead
Dead Center
Sudden Death
Bury the Lead
First Degree
Open and Shut

K TEAM NOVELS

Good Dog, Bad Cop
Citizen K-9
Animal Instinct
The K Team

THRILLERS

Black and Blue
Fade to Black
Blackout
Without Warning
Airtight
Heart of a Killer
On Borrowed Time
Down to the Wire
Don't Tell a Soul

NONFICTION

Lessons from Tara: Life Advice from the World's Most Brilliant Dog

Dogtripping: 25 Rescues, 11 Volunteers, and 3 RVs on Our Canine Cross-Country Adventure

THE MORE THE TERRIER

David Rosenfelt

MINOTAUR BOOKS
NEW YORK

This is a work of fiction. All of the characters, organizations, and events portrayed in this novel are either products of the author's imagination or are used fictitiously.

First published in the United States by Minotaur Books, an imprint of St. Martin's Publishing Group

For information, address St. Martin's Publishing Group, 120 Broadway, New York, NY 10271.

www.minotaurbooks.com

The Library of Congress Cataloging-in-Publication Data is available upon request.

ISBN 978-1-250-32454-2 (hardcover)
ISBN 978-1-250-32455-9 (ebook)

First Edition: 2024

10 9 8 7 6 5 4 3 2 1

THE MORE THE TERRIER

Professor Steven Rayburn had not been looking forward to this night.

He was not a fan of confrontation, and he had considered avoiding this one, but recent events had left him no choice. He knew what he had to do, even if doing it would be extremely unpleasant.

It had turned out even worse than he expected. There were no regrets from the other person, no offer of contrition or any type of compromise. Not that compromise was possible; Rayburn was not going to have any of it.

When the other person finally left, at seven thirty, Rayburn took a deep breath and headed for the den to pour himself a drink. The next steps would be important; he had to follow through and do what he had vowed to do, even though he would take no pleasure in it.

What Rayburn didn't realize was that the person had not actually left, only simulated it by opening and closing the front door, then remained in the house and moved quietly toward the living room.

It is unlikely that Rayburn ever realized he was not alone. Perhaps he did in a nanosecond of consciousness when the metal statue was smashed into his head, but that can never be known.

What is known for sure is that Professor Steven Rayburn was dead before his body hit the floor.

I'm not a winter person.

I don't like very cold weather, which doesn't really set me apart from most people I know. Cold is the reason they invented furnaces, and fireplaces, and heavy coats.

I also stopped hoping for snow at around the time it stopped getting me an off day from school. It's pretty while it's falling, but where I live, in Paterson, New Jersey, it gets dirty and ugly on the ground and stays that way for days. It can also turn so icy that the best way to get around town would be on a Zamboni.

I don't like skiing, or at least I'm pretty sure I wouldn't like it if I ever tried it. I can't understand why anyone would want to barrel down a frozen mountain at high speed on two narrow ironing boards, carrying a couple of sticks and dodging trees and other lunatics out on the same mountain. Then, if you survive intact, you get lifted to the top of the mountain on a thin cable, just so you can defy death again.

As best as I can tell, a good day on the slopes is not suffering broken bones, frostbite, or worse, which is why I have spent many good days in front of the television, or reading a book. You never hear about a medevac helicopter picking someone up from their den and flying them to a trauma center.

Winter does have football, which is a major plus . . . I'll give it that.

Of course, I'm not a summer person either. Summer is the reason they had to invent air-conditioning and swimming and bug spray. Lying on a beach is as nutty as skiing; the trick there is to cover yourself with so much grease that you don't get skin cancer while you bake. Another way to avoid it would be not to bake at all.

There is much I don't like about the heat of summer, but suffice it to say that I'm opposed to any weather in which mosquitoes thrive.

There are maybe four or five days a year that measure up to my exacting weather standards . . . they usually happen in early May or mid-September. My wife, Laurie Collins, sometimes comments on my complaints about the weather. Her view is that I am a pain in the ass, or at least that's how she puts it.

But I can now report that it's possible I am changing. I have spent the last five days in what some people would describe as a winter wonderland. Laurie and I are at a resort in the Adirondacks with our fifteen-year-old son, Ricky. Also here are Brian and Sally Rubenstein and their son, Will, who is Ricky's best friend.

Much to Laurie's surprise, I have become Andy Carpenter, Outdoorsman. We've all gone ice-skating and snowmobiling and even sledding. I haven't gone skiing, mainly because my brain is not completely frozen.

But I've been out there doing stuff and I don't have a

single broken bone or frostbitten toe to show for it. And in the off-hours, I've been sitting in front of the fireplace and sucking down hot chocolate. Not a bad way to spend some time.

The only real negative is that Christmas music has played constantly throughout the hotel. Since Laurie thinks the Christmas season starts around Halloween, I have long ago passed my tolerance level for that gooey musical junk. I don't care that "it's Christmastime in the city." We're here to get away from the city.

This morning we had a predeparture snowball fight, the adults against the kids. We adults came in second and it wasn't close.

All in all, we had a great time, diminished only by Laurie's insistence that we listen to the "Jolly Christmas" station on satellite radio all the way home. By the tenth time a singer asked, "Sleigh bells ring, are you listening?," I wanted to scream, "Yes, I'm listening! I have no choice! Stop asking me!"

But now we're almost home, and I'm very much looking forward to seeing our three dogs. There is Tara, a golden retriever who has permanently retired the Best Dog in the Universe trophy. Then there's Hunter, a pug who understandably worships Tara and follows her everywhere. And lastly there's Sebastian, a basset hound who is built like a combination washer-dryer and has the energy level of that same washer-dryer when it is unplugged.

We don't travel much, and I hate being away from the dogs. Tara and I have been a team for a very long time; the other two are relatively recent additions. Tara has seen me through some tough times, asking only for petting and biscuits in return.

Taking care of them this week has been the amazing Jenny Bedell, our friend and occasional dog sitter. She lives at the house and gives them even better care than we do while she does, which is saying a lot. She also keeps us constantly informed by text about how they are doing, including photos.

I can hear the barking as soon as we pull into the driveway. We live on Forty-second Street in Paterson, New Jersey, and our neighbors are close by. They've never complained about the barking, possibly because most of them have dogs of their own. It's a very canine-friendly neighborhood.

When we walk in, Jenny is standing across from the front door with the dogs, who get wildly excited and charge toward us. Just before I happily fall to the ground covered in dogs, I realize something surprising.

There aren't three dogs.

There are four.

He showed up at the front door two days ago and wouldn't leave," Jenny says about the little dog, who looks like a Yorkie mix."I didn't want to take him to the shelter, and I knew for sure you wouldn't want me to. At first I fed him out on the porch, but it was cold, so I brought him inside. I didn't know what else to do. I hope it's okay; he seems really sweet."

"You did fine," Laurie says, a sentiment with which I agree.

"I'm glad to hear you say that," Jenny says. "I put up signs around the neighborhood, but nobody has contacted me. I didn't tell you about it because I figured there was nothing you could do, and you'd find out soon enough."

"No tags on him?" I ask.

"No. I sent my cousin a picture of him. She's very much a dog person, and she thinks he's a terrier mix."

"Could be," Laurie says.

"We need to find out if he's chipped. There's a scanner at the foundation." I'm referring to the Tara Foundation, a rescue group that my friends Willie and Sondra Miller run with me. They do most of the "running," especially when I have a case in my other, less enjoyable life as a criminal defense attorney.

"What do we do if he's not chipped?" Laurie asks.

"We'll keep him at the foundation. I'll alert the shelter that if anyone comes looking for a dog matching his description, they can send them to us. If they can prove that they're his owners, then they'll get him. If nobody shows up in the next week, we'll find him a great home."

"You know, he looks like Murphy," Laurie says. "With more hair."

We once rescued a dog named Murphy, who had a terrible skin condition. He wasn't doing well at the foundation, so we brought him home and treated him for it while he lived with us. The process took about eight weeks, and then we placed him in a terrific home with a woman and her teenaged son. This was about two years ago.

Ricky, who is busy petting Tara, hears Laurie and says, "Is that Murphy?" He and Murphy had bonded during his time with us.

"No," Laurie says. "It just looks like him."

Ricky goes over to the dog and says, "The Giants won."

The dog goes crazy, literally jumping up and down on his hind legs. "It's him!" Ricky yells, because that is a trick he taught Murphy when he was here. Ricky runs into the kitchen and comes back with a biscuit, which was always the reward when Murphy did the trick.

Laurie and I both stare with our mouths open. "Could that be him?" she asks.

"Unless we happen to have found another terrier mix

who's a Giants fan," I say. "Which would be a surprise, because terriers generally like winners."

"That's Murphy!" Ricky says, and I'm thinking he could be right.

"Maybe he got lost, remembered this house, and showed up. That's why he wouldn't leave," Laurie says.

"It's possible," I say. "I'm going to take him down and get him scanned."

We chip every dog that comes into the foundation, and then the adopters change the name and address that the chip reveals. So if this is somehow Murphy, we'll know soon enough.

I bring Ricky and the mystery dog down to the foundation. Sondra is out, but as soon as Willie sees the dog he says, "That dog looks familiar."

"That's why we want to scan him," I say, and we go into the back room where the machine is.

The dog is smiling throughout this process; whatever he thinks is going on, he likes the attention.

Willie runs the scanning device and it beeps, indicating that there is in fact a chip. He then looks at the readout and says, "Damn, that's Murphy."

"I told you," Ricky says.

The chip scan shows Murphy's owner to be Doris Bremer, who lives in Paterson, about fifteen minutes from my house.

I'm pretty sure that I recognize the name; I think she was the one who adopted him, along with her teenage son. If I remember correctly, his name is BJ. BJ spent quite a bit of time at our house petting and taking care of Murphy. He was a terrific kid and a real dog lover.

Willie gets out the records and my recollection is confirmed; the adopter was indeed Doris Bremer. I am guessing that Murphy somehow ran off and got disoriented, finally realizing he was near our house, which he recognized and remembered from his stay with us.

This probably happened recently because Murphy looks well cared for. I doubt he spent a lot of time scavenging as a stray on the street. At least I hope not; the nights get really cold this time of year.

The address on the chip is the same as the one in our records, so Willie comes with me as we go to her house to talk to them about returning Murphy. We first drop Ricky off at home; I don't know for sure why Murphy was running loose, but I instinctively don't want Ricky there when we find out.

When we get to the Bremer house, there is a car in the driveway and I can see a light on inside the house. Murphy perks up noticeably when he realizes where we are, though perky is pretty much his default position. Murphy is the type of dog that brightens up every room and car he is in.

We get out of the car and Willie takes Murphy out of the backseat. In the front window of the house, I can see Doris Bremer looking out the window at us. After a few moments, she disappears from the window and the front door opens. She comes out on the porch and says, "Oh, my God . . ."

She's crying.

I'm not a big fan of women crying, or actually of anyone crying. I never know what to say or do. I usually try to defuse it with some kind of joke, which literally never works. People who are crying are not usually receptive to humor, at least not mine.

"I believe you know Mr. Murphy?" I ask, and that moves her from quiet crying to open sobbing. *Good job, Andy.*

"Come in, come in," she finally manages, hugging Murphy and still crying. "God, I have been so worried."

We follow her inside and into the den and she asks us to sit. We do so, and she leaves the room, with Murphy following her.

Willie and I just look at each other, not knowing why we're sitting here, and after a few minutes Doris comes back with a tray of delicious-looking muffins and cookies and a pot of coffee.

"You just whip that up, did you?" I ask.

She smiles, but it's a sad smile. "When I'm upset, I bake for the whole neighborhood. I'm diabetic so really can't eat it myself."

"Upset about losing Murphy?" I ask, taking a bite of what can only be described as an extraordinarily delicious blueberry muffin.

She nods. "That too. I must have accidentally left the door open one day, and I suppose he ran off and couldn't find his way back. I looked everywhere."

"When was this?" Willie asks.

"Maybe a week ago? The days seem to be blending together lately. Each one is worse than the day before."

She's starting to choke up again. I'm sorry for her, but that feeling is competing with my desire to get out of here. It's a close match, but the get-out-of-here desire is winning. That's no surprise; in cases like this, get-out-of-here is undefeated.

I'm also starting to think that her level of upset is about more than just Murphy, especially since she said "that too" when I asked her if she was upset about him. But it's really not my business, and I don't want to pry. So I opt for small talk before making our exit. "How's BJ?"

I must not be a great small-talker either, because it starts the tears flowing full force again. "He's not home" is all she can muster.

I want to leave it there, but Willie obviously thinks otherwise. Discretion is not Willie's strong point, and, as did I, he also liked BJ during the adoption and post-adoption process. "Where is he?" he asks.

"He's in jail. They took him away."

Willie again. "Why?"

"They said he killed someone, a teacher. You know my BJ; he could never hurt anyone. It's all so horrible and unbelievable, like a nightmare that never ends." Then she grabs Murphy and hugs him. "I was so afraid to tell him that Murphy was gone. He loves this dog so much. I can never thank you enough for bringing him back to me."

I take out a card and hand it to her. "Doris, if you need anything, anything at all, you call me, okay?"

"You brought back Murphy."

"Yes, but if you need anything else . . ."

"Thank you."

I smile. "And keep the door closed. We don't want Murphy getting out again."

"I will. Thank you so much."

We leave, and I confess I selfishly and pathetically grab a muffin on the way out. Once we're outside, Willie says, "No way BJ killed anyone."

Willie was himself imprisoned for a murder he did not commit, so he is keenly aware of the potential for mistakes to be made.

"He sure didn't seem like the type," I say.

"He didn't do it."

"You've seen the evidence?"

"I don't need to. He didn't do it."

"Willie, I wish I had you on some of my juries."

I drop Willie off and head home.

On the way, I can predict how the upcoming scene will play out as clearly as if I was pressing Play on a DVD of a movie I've already seen. I'm not even sure if DVDs are still a thing; it seems like they had a shelf life of about an hour, sandwiched between VHS tapes and streaming.

I can see the scene unfold in my mind as if I am Marty Scorsese. I will tell Laurie about our conversation with Doris Bremer, and she will suggest I look into BJ's situation, to see if I can help. She will do this because she liked BJ and because she is a decent person.

She knows that I do not want to take on any clients and that my instinct is to not get involved, but her basic goodness will overcome that.

Basic goodness is an overrated quality.

Of course, there is one way to rewrite the scene. I can tell her only that we returned Murphy to a grateful Doris Bremer and that he is now home safely. That would be entirely true and would get me off the hook. If I wanted, I could then check out BJ's situation with no pressure, without that basic-goodness thing hovering over me.

The more I think about it, it sounds like a good plan,

with few flaws. But Mike Tyson once said that everybody coming into a fight has a good plan until they get punched in the mouth. I imagine Laurie strapping on the gloves and waiting for me to get home.

"You took Murphy home?" she asks. For this performance, the role of Mike Tyson is being played by Laurie Collins.

"Yup. Sure did. Took old Murphy right on home. Murphy's home; yes, he is." I'm babbling already and I just got here.

"I'll bet Mrs. Bremer and BJ were happy to get him back."

I nod; I'm already on shaky ground. "A lot of tears, that's for sure. They were flowing."

"Is BJ home, or at school? Rutgers, wasn't it?"

"No, he wasn't home, and he's not at old Rutgers."

"Where is he?" She might as well have said, "Checkmate."

"BJ is in jail," I say, in the way a cornered rat might say it. Bottom line . . . I just got punched in the mouth.

"In jail? I don't understand."

Now that the die is cast, I tell Laurie exactly what Doris Bremer said. Laurie's response is "That does not sound like BJ. Andy, we need to look into this."

Laurie is a former cop and one of my investigators in my practice, so when she says "we," she means it. I'm playing a losing hand here.

But I'm going down fighting. "Laurie, you know I do not want or need a client." It seems like I have been saying this forever; we have plenty of money, more than we'll ever need, and I have no desire to plunge into a murder case. "I would rather spend the next few months skiing."

"I know, Andy, but it's Christmas."

"Oh, I forgot. One of the traditions of Christmas is that lawyers have to take on cases they don't want. It's like the potential client rubs a Christmas tree and the lawyer-genie pops out."

"Andy . . ." She says that one word in a way that is more powerful than my whole speech. I'm not sure how she does it; she must have majored in speech inflection in college.

"Okay," I say, my defeat already certain. "We'll look into it."

Fortunately, Google has already looked into it, and I can read about the case online. Last month a visiting computer science professor at Rutgers, Steven Rayburn, was murdered in his home. The police arrested Brian Bremer, a student of Rayburn's, and described it as a robbery attempt gone bad.

I sort of remember reading about it, but since I knew Brian only as BJ, I never made the connection.

There is no mention made in the stories of Brian's current legal status other than to say he has been charged with first-degree murder and arraigned in Middlesex County, which is where Rutgers is located.

I'm not sure how Middlesex County got its name; supposedly it had to do with Anglo-Saxons in England. But I have my doubts; why name a New Jersey county after some people in a foreign country more than a thousand years ago? I would not discount the possibility that there was a fun-loving county clerk with naming responsibilities.

The stories mention that BJ is being represented by a lawyer named James Howarth. I've never heard of Mr. Howarth, which is no surprise. I know a lot of defense attorneys here in Passaic County, but I've only had one previous case in Middlesex, so I'm not familiar with the players there.

Based on the article, it doesn't appear as if Mr. Howarth is a public defender, which sort of surprises me. Murder cases are expensive to try; it's hard for me to picture Doris Bremer having that kind of money.

There is just not enough detail here to know what is going on in the case, and obviously nothing that would indicate BJ's guilt or innocence. The police clearly believe he is guilty, and, more important, the prosecutor believes he can prove it to a jury.

It's Mr. Howarth's job, and mine when I am forced to work, to show that at the very least there is reasonable doubt about that guilt.

I call Sam Willis, who is my accountant in real life, but who morphs into Super-Hacker when I have a case. Sam can hack into anything, legally or otherwise, and that has earned him a place as a valuable investigator on our team.

He would rather be "on the street," as he calls it, doing what he considers real detective work. He even got a license to carry a gun, just in case. But not only is he more valuable to me behind a keyboard, if he was "on the street," he would probably shoot himself.

I tell him to go online and see what he can find out

about the murder of Professor Rayburn, and BJ's accused involvement in it.

"We have a case?" he asks, in such a way that I can picture him salivating over the phone. "And it's Rayburn?"

"No. Just checking something out." Then, "Did you know Rayburn?"

"I knew of him. He was a star in the computer world." He promises to get on it, but I can't imagine he'll find anything that will satisfy me, and certainly not Laurie.

I'm going to have to go see BJ.

Mike Tyson was right.

Middlesex County is not going to run out of Brunswicks anytime soon.

There is East Brunswick, North Brunswick, South Brunswick, and New Brunswick. I have no idea why they stopped there and didn't add a West Brunswick or an Old Brunswick; these are the kind of governmental decisions I find confounding.

There actually is a West Brunswick in Somerset County, but there is also a place there called Peapack and Gladstone, which is a sign that Somerset was pretty desperate for acceptable names.

North Brunswick is where the Middlesex jail is, so that's where I'm going. I had Eddie Dowd, the other lawyer in our mini-firm, call ahead and set up the okay for my visit. I'm sure they'll make me wait anyway, since that's part of the annoying process, but hopefully it won't be too bad.

It turns out not to be bad at all; by jail standards the twenty-minute wait is short for a defense attorney. Maybe it is quicker this time because Eddie had me listed as a friend of BJ's, not his attorney.

They bring me into a meeting room that is the same as every other meeting room in every jail I've ever been in. Another five minutes go by before BJ is brought in. He looks thinner than I remember; I don't know if that's a result of this ordeal or if he just lost weight in the two years since I've seen him.

He looks at me strangely, as if he's trying to make the connection. "Mr. Carpenter? Andy?"

Clearly no one told him I was coming. "Hello, BJ," I say, which he will probably take as confirmation of my identity.

"I don't understand; what are you doing here?" Then I can see concern sweep across his face, and he asks, "Has anything happened to Murphy?"

"Murphy's fine; he's with your mother. I'm here because I'm interested in your case."

"Thank you. I don't really know what to say. It's horrible. I didn't do what they say; I could never do anything like that. My lawyer tells me he can make a deal; he thinks I should. But it would mean prison for most of my life. I can't do that; I just can't."

"I understand."

"Mr. Carpenter, do you know a different lawyer that maybe I could talk to? Somebody who might believe me? I'm pretty sure Mr. Howarth thinks I'm guilty."

Apparently the Andy Carpenter fame is not as widespread as I thought. "I'm a defense attorney, BJ."

"You are?"

"Yes. How did you come to hire Mr. Howarth?"

"I'm not sure; he visited me at the jail and said he would help me. That he believed my story."

"Did you pay him?"

"No."

"Okay. Why don't you just tell me what happened?"

"I don't really know for sure; I mean, I know my part of it. There's this professor, Professor Rayburn, he taught a computer class I'm taking. I was taking . . ."

BJ shakes his head, no doubt at the jarring remembrance of how much in his life has changed. Then he continues, "I didn't like him very much; he was sort of arrogant, you know? But he was a brilliant guy; beyond brilliant."

I'm torn between wanting to speed this up and knowing I should let him tell it at his own pace. I opt for his own pace.

"We had an argument in class one day; he gave me a C on a paper that should have been an A. He said an answer I gave was wrong, but it was actually correct, and I pointed out how. He didn't agree with me, or maybe he didn't want to admit I was right, and I got angry and argued with him about it."

"In front of your classmates?"

BJ nods. "Yeah. Then a couple of days later I got a phone call from the department clerk telling me that Professor Rayburn wanted me to come to his house that evening to discuss my situation. I asked what it was about, but he said he didn't know.

"I was afraid Rayburn was going to flunk me or something, or maybe report me for insubordination. The guy was a pain in the ass, and he sure as hell did not like to be challenged.

"I thought going to his house was weird; I mean, he had an office on campus. But I couldn't say no, so I went."

"What happened when you got there?"

"The door was open, and—"

"You mean unlocked?"

"No, open. Like a couple of feet. I called out, but nobody answered. So I poked my head in and looked inside. He was on the floor, across this sort of large foyer that he had. I thought I saw something next to him; it seemed like it could have been blood."

"What did you do?"

"I went in to see if I could help. There was a lot of blood, it started down the hallway and ended up where he was. His head was . . . it was horrible."

"What did you do next?"

"I grabbed for my phone to call nine-one-one, but before I could, police came through the door. They had guns and they were screaming for me to get down on the floor."

"Did you have any blood on you?"

BJ nods. "Yes, there was some there when I got down on the ground. I did it so fast because I was scared, so I wasn't careful. I told them I didn't do anything, that I just found him like that, but I don't think they believed me. But they let me go."

"When did they arrest you?"

"The next morning. They came to my apartment with a search warrant and had me wait outside in one of their cars. Then they came out with a watch and some money and asked how it came to be there. I said it wasn't there, that I never saw it before. They handcuffed me and took me to the precinct."

"Did they read you your rights?"

"Yes, and they told me I was entitled to a lawyer. But I didn't know any." Then, "Will you help me? I don't trust Howarth, and I think he lied about believing me."

"I'll look into it further; that's the best I can promise for now."

"I understand. Thank you. If I ever get back there, do you think I'd still have my scholarship? My mother could never afford to send me, even though it's a state school."

"Yes, if you get back there, I believe you will still have your scholarship. There would be no reason to take it away."

He nods. "Good." Then, "Have you seen Murphy?"

"Yes; he's doing very well. Your mom is taking good care of him."

"I knew she would. They wouldn't let me keep him in the apartment I was assigned, so I was hoping to move next year. Now . . ."

"One step at a time, BJ. One step at a time."

"Obviously I can't share conversations I've had with BJ. Client confidentiality," James Howarth says.

"I'm familiar with the concept," I say, "and it's fine; I wouldn't want you to."

"You're a friend of the family?"

"Yes. A close friend. And you also don't need to tell me what he said because I've already spoken with him. He says you've raised the possibility of a plea deal and suggested that he take it."

I'm in Howarth's office, which is in a strip mall in East Brunswick between a barbershop and a 7-Eleven. I'm not saying this as an elitist; my office is even more of a dump than this, but Howarth is clearly not an attorney to the stars.

He nods. "The prosecutor offered forty to life, with possibility of parole after thirty. It's no walk in the park, but in BJ's case he could be out at fifty. Lot of life ahead of him after that."

"He's not interested in a deal. Which I'm sure he told you."

"Yes, he did. For now."

"So you do think he should take it?"

"It's his call, but he'll get worse if he's convicted."

"Did his mother hire you?"

"No."

"So who is paying your fee?"

Howarth immediately looks wary. "That is not something I am going to share with you."

"Do you think he's guilty?" It's not a question I usually ask, but this is an unusual situation and conversation. I'm not getting the feeling I'm sitting across from Clarence Darrow; nor do I think I'm talking to someone who cares about BJ.

Howarth shrugs. "I think there's a strong case against him."

"Where does it stand now?"

"He's been arraigned and pleaded not guilty. A trial date has been set and I have the discovery. What is your interest in this, beyond being a friend of the family?"

I come to the decision in the moment. "I'm his new attorney. Which makes you his former attorney. You can consider yourself relieved of the assignment, effective with the conclusion of this sentence."

"That's bullshit. You can't move in on me like that; it's not ethical."

"You concern yourself with ethics a lot, do you?"

"You're damn right, and I don't like what you're implying. And why would you want to take on a sure-loser case?"

I ignore the question. "I'll draw up a letter for BJ to sign to make it official. I'm guessing you don't have investigative work product to turn over to me?"

"You do your own investigating."

I hadn't come here having made a decision to take the case, but there's no way I can leave BJ with this creep. Everything about him gets on my nerves. And I very much want to know how he came to be BJ's lawyer; this is not a guy who fights for truth and justice pro bono.

"It's been a treat chatting with you," I say.

I leave and then stop back at the jail to tell BJ that I will take his case. After I had left, he had used the hour of computer time that he is granted to look me up.

"You're an amazing lawyer," he says. "I had no idea."

"Aw, shucks, enough about me. Did Howarth tell you not to talk to anyone here about anything having to do with your case?"

"No."

"Figures. Well, I'm telling you. Not a word to anyone. You talk to me only. Understood?"

"Understood." Then, "This is amazing. I thought all you did was rescue dogs."

"Someday, BJ. Someday."

I've always felt that the first few days of an investigation are the most important.

Certainly police detectives also consider that to be the case, but I find it's equally true for the defense.

In that way it's probably like a serious medical event. You always hear that in the case of a heart attack or stroke, the speed and effectiveness of the initial treatment sets the tone. It's the same way with a trial; if the defense falls behind early on, it can spend the entire case on life support.

It's obviously too late for us to get back the time we missed; the days right after the murder and the arrest are long past. But that doesn't mean we shouldn't move quickly and get right into gear; we have a lot of time to make up.

My first call when I leave the jail is to Laurie, to tell her to notify our team and set up our initial meeting.

"You took the case already?" she asks, obviously surprised.

"Of course. How often do cases with endless hours of work, very little chance to win, and no money come along? How could I turn it down?"

She laughs. "This could make your career. If you win, you'll be a client magnet."

I say that I will call Eddie Dowd myself; I want him to make sure that Howarth transfers the discovery documents to us immediately. Eddie is a lawyer who works with me when we have a case, and he can be very persuasive about things like this. I also ask Eddie to contact the prosecution and the court and notify them of the change in BJ's representation.

Eddie says he will do all of that promptly, which means I can put it into the metaphorical "done" file. Eddie is completely reliable, and just as competent. Plus, because he is a former tight end for the New York Giants, people know him and take him seriously.

When I get home, I take the dogs for a walk, and Laurie joins me. Ricky has gone over to Will Rubenstein's; apparently spending all that time together in the Adirondacks has not diminished their friendship.

Because I haven't walked them in a while, we take the dogs on a long one, through Eastside Park, starting at the Park Avenue end and then all the way to the Broadway side, and then back.

We only take Tara and Hunter; Sebastian has long ago made it clear that he thinks walking is for suckers. Sebastian prefers to stroll around our backyard to get in his "exercise" and do his business. I don't think Sebastian would be much of a skier either.

On the way I tell Laurie about my meetings with BJ and Howarth.

"BJ must be so scared," she says.

I nod. "That definitely came across. And if he wasn't scared, then we should be planning an insanity defense. His entire life is in front of him."

"Do you think he could have done this?"

"I can't say otherwise; I don't know him nearly well enough to be sure of his innocence. But I have a good feeling about him, so we'll see."

"It's great of you to do this."

"It's Christmas," I say. "Which reminds me, is anybody on the team away for the holidays?"

"No, all available and ready to go. I set the meeting for ten o'clock tomorrow at the house. It's more festive."

My office is a dump above a fruit stand on Van Houten Street in downtown Paterson. I haven't been there in a while and certainly have made no effort to liven up the place. BJ's cell is probably more festive.

On the other hand, his cell wouldn't have the incessant Christmas music that Laurie plays around the clock. The jailers are missing an opportunity; they could use constant playing of that music to get prisoners to confess.

When we get home, Eddie calls to tell me that the prosecutor on the case is Timothy Nabers. The name means nothing to me; since I don't try cases in Middlesex County, I am not familiar with the prosecutors there.

"The word is that he's excellent. Focused and always very well prepared," Eddie says.

"Super."

Each member of our team comes into the initial case meeting with a predictable mindset.

For the most part they are different from one another, but they never change from case to case. As they gather in our den this morning, I can tell what they're thinking. I wish I could read jurors' minds this easily.

Sam Willis is obvious. He's thrilled to be involved, which makes sense. He's an accountant, which tends to make everything else seem exciting. He knows that his work on this case will be confined to his considerable computer skills, but he's secretly hoping for something more. He's going to be disappointed; I will chain him to his keyboard if I have to.

Corey Douglas, an ex-cop who is one of Laurie's partners in an investigating firm, is skeptical. Because of his training and background, his natural assumption is that if a person is charged with a crime, he or she is likely guilty of that crime. It's far from an ideal attitude for someone working for the defense, but he is able to put that aside and do the work.

Corey's partner on the force and fellow retiree, Simon Garfunkel, is in the other room playing with Tara. That's okay, because Simon is a German shepherd. When called upon, Simon has no trouble displaying his considerable crime-fighting talents, but he also seems to enjoy retirement. I fully understand that.

Laurie, also being an ex-cop, has always had an attitude similar to Corey's, but it has diminished over time. I think my point of view in distrusting the prosecution's theories might be growing on her, though she would never admit it. One thing she would admit is that she supports me 100 percent, and that attitude is certainly reciprocated. She also absolutely wants to do everything she can for BJ.

Eddie Dowd is all-business. He plows ahead relentlessly on any assignment given, and his tenaciousness is matched by his smarts. Eddie is eager but realistic; he knows that our role is to challenge the system and make sure it works as it should. Whether that leads to a just outcome is not the point; we do our job and then the chips fall where they may.

The person least happy to be here is my office manager and assistant, Edna. Edna is fine with part of her job, but not with all of it. She's good with cashing paychecks, but not so much with doing actual work. Her preferred outcome on our cases, before she even knows what they're about, is to broker a plea bargain and end it. She should probably work for James Howarth.

She recently split with her fiancé, a retired fast-food executive, when they couldn't decide on a location for their planned destination wedding. That has made her even less inclined to work, but more anxious to be paid. I go along with this because I like Edna, and because I am clearly an idiot.

Marcus Clark is the one exception regarding my mind-reading talents. I never know what is going on in Marcus's mind, except for the certainty that it does not include anything resembling fear. Fear is reserved for those around him.

Marcus is to scary what Edna is to lazy. He is also incredibly powerful and violent when the situation calls for it, and the situation often calls for it. But he is on our side, something I am thankful for every minute of every day. If it wasn't for Marcus's frequent interventions, I would be trying cases in that great courtroom in the sky.

Except for Edna, I am the least happy to be here. I know that until the trial, if there is one, I am going to be obsessed with the case and will be working when I'd rather be napping or watching football.

Back in the day I was worried about flunking out of law school when I should have been embracing the idea.

"Our client is Brian Bremer; we know him by his nickname of BJ," I say. "He's nineteen years old and is a computer science student at Rutgers. He is accused of murdering a Rutgers professor named Steven Rayburn.

"Professor Rayburn was killed by blunt-force trauma; he was hit over the head with a metal sculpture that was in his home. There were signs of a robbery in the house, though I don't at this point know whether anything was actually taken.

"I know very little about the specifics of the case right now, as we are awaiting the transfer of the discovery from his previous lawyer in Middlesex County. Our client says that he was summoned to the professor's house, probably to discuss a dispute they had over a grade. When he arrived, he found the body."

"Was the dispute public?" Corey asks.

"Yes. The argument apparently happened in class. BJ thought he was being unfairly treated in that an answer he gave was correct and it was marked wrong. He tried to point this out to Professor Rayburn, but got nowhere."

"Motive?" Corey says.

"We will need to do a deep dive on Professor Rayburn to find out who else might have had an interest in killing him. Obviously, if it was a random robbery gone bad, we have a bigger problem in that there will be nothing about Rayburn's life that could help identify his killer.

"Sam has already gotten started on Rayburn, and hopefully the discovery will open up new directions. The rest of you will have to wait until we have a better feel for the case. It won't be long, and once we get going, it will have to be at top speed. We've lost a lot of time."

"Will do," Sam says. "Anything else?"

"Yes. BJ was being represented by a guy named James Howarth; he has an office in East Brunswick. He is a slimeball extraordinaire, and he was getting paid from someone other than the Bremers. I want to know anything you can find out about him, including who was paying him."

"I know a bunch of Middlesex cops," Corey says. "I can ask around there as well."

"Good. Can't hurt."

"Do you want to try for a change of venue?" Eddie asks.

"Rutgers is a pretty big deal down there; it employs a lot of people."

"Seems flimsy," I say, "but can't hurt to try. It would be nice not to have to make that drive every day. On the other hand, the Middlesex judges don't know me well enough to hate me."

"Any chance for a plea bargain?" Edna asks.

"He's already turned it down," I say, and I can see Edna sag slightly in disappointment. "Okay, everybody, that's a wrap for now."

Discovery documents make depressing reading for defense attorneys.

That's stating the obvious, since what they contain has led to the client's being charged for the crime. So it's all bad stuff; there is no way that the opening line will be "Great news! Your client is innocent; we were nuts to charge him. Our bad."

The documents do have their upside, which is the only reason I don't set fire to them. By telling us how the police have built their case, they provide a road map to attacking it. That is easier said than done, but the fact that nothing the prosecution will present will come as a surprise is invaluable to our side.

The second paragraph on the first document is particularly ominous. It says that BJ was arrested in his apartment at eight o'clock on the morning after the murder, which was only twelve hours after the body was discovered.

Always leery of the inevitable claim by the defense that the police rushed to judgment, in this case they were clearly confident that their case was strong enough to withstand such a charge.

They are certainly correct in that assessment. As I read

on, it's clear that the evidence more than justified the arrest. That's not to say that the evidence is immune to challenge; I won't know that until we have had a chance to investigate it thoroughly. But just based on what the cops had in front of them, there is no doubt that the arrest was warranted.

The police received a phone call at just around eight the previous night from an anonymous person who identified himself as a neighbor of Professor Rayburn's. He said that it sounded like there was violence in the house, that two people were screaming at each other, and there were sounds of things being thrown around.

The Rutgers campus police responded within minutes, followed by New Brunswick officers. When they arrived, they found BJ standing near Rayburn's dead body. His head was crushed, and it was later learned that the murder weapon was a metal statue. There were no fingerprints on the statue; there was evidence that it was wiped clean with a paper towel that was on the floor nearby. But BJ did have some blood on his hand, clothing, and shoes.

BJ gave a statement at the scene. He said that he had received a call from a clerk in the computer science department, who said that Rayburn wanted to see him at his house at eight that night, to discuss a class matter. He stated that he thought that was unusual, but that he certainly never considered refusing to comply.

He told the police the same story he told me, that he discovered the body and was about to call 911 when the cops arrived. He said that he did not see anyone leaving the scene and had no relevant information that he could give them as to who the perpetrator might have been.

The house was ransacked; most notably Rayburn's computer was smashed. It was difficult for the police to tell what might have been stolen since they had no way of knowing what possessions Rayburn had prior to the event.

The police did not take BJ into custody that night, but secured a search warrant for his car and apartment. The subsequent search of his apartment found a Rolex watch and $642 in cash, apparently hidden in a jacket pocket in his closet.

They determined that the watch had belonged to Professor Rayburn and made the arrest. BJ denied any knowledge of the watch or money and claimed that none of it should have been in his apartment.

The case is obviously strong. They have motive, although I think it's a bit flimsy. I disagreed with professors a number of times over grades, but can't ever remember hitting one over the head with a statue. But they also have BJ's presence on the scene and stolen merchandise in his apartment.

The one positive thing in the discovery, at least from our perspective, is that the autopsy found recreational drugs in Rayburn's blood. It was determined that he had taken those drugs relatively recently, which means in the forty-eight hours before he died.

But the bottom line is that there are two possibilities here. One is that the cops are correct and BJ is guilty. The other is that the real murderer set it up to look as if BJ is guilty. The Rolex and money didn't walk to his apartment by themselves; either BJ put them there or someone else planted them.

We have to take the position that our client is innocent, which means we must point to someone else as a reasonable possibility to have committed the murder. It's either BJ or a still-unknown person . . . one or the other.

Identifying murderers is a zero-sum game.

Rutgers has an interesting decision to make regarding the murder scene.

It's a nice house not far off campus, befitting a faculty member of significant status. I read in the discovery that Rutgers provided it to Professor Rayburn at minimum cost; they have a number of other houses that serve a similar purpose.

But this one saw the occupant's head bashed in, which is not necessarily something that would appeal to the next professor coming down the pike. I suppose Rutgers could truthfully say that every professor who has stayed there has enjoyed the experience, with the exception of one.

Laurie and I visit every murder scene at the beginning of a case, and we're here today to continue the tradition. Of course it's a bit different in this instance, since the crime happened quite a while ago.

There are no police present anymore; I am sure they haven't been here in a while. Forensics has long ago done its work.

The cops promised that the door would be open when we got here, and in fact it is. We enter to find that the place has been cleaned up. Where there had been blood and brain matter splattered all over, the tile is now clean and sparkling.

I'm not sure where Professor Rayburn's possessions are, but they are no longer here. The place shows no sign of habitation whatsoever; it's just waiting for the next person to come along.

We know from the photographs in the discovery where the key event took place. Laurie points to the hallway and says, "That's where he was struck. The blood trail began there."

I nod. "And he was hit from behind, which is why he went forward to there, where he fell." I point to a spot at the entrance to the den.

"It's hard to know if he was surprised by someone coming up behind him, or if he was walking or running away from his assailant."

"Probably the latter. It would be hard to walk on this floor without making noise. He likely would have turned if he heard someone sneaking up on him."

She points. "The person could have been hiding in that doorway. Then Rayburn would not have heard him approach."

"Possible."

"Where was the statue that he was hit with? Do the police say where the killer picked it up?"

"In the living room, which is down that hall."

"It feels to me like he wasn't surprised by an intruder," she says. "That he knew the killer and spent at least a little time with him before he was hit."

"I agree, but it's hard to be sure. And of course I would

prefer the intruder theory. BJ was invited to meet with him."

Laurie walks over to the front window. "So BJ's car was parked out there, and I assume he came in this front door."

I nod. "As did the police."

"So their theory is that he killed Rayburn, stole the watch and some money, went out to put it in his car, and then came back in?"

"Right. And then he hid it in his apartment when he got home. And they figured he came back in so he could say, as he did, that he found the professor already dead and was calling the police."

We walk around the house, checking out the living room, bedrooms, and office. Some of them had been either vandalized or robbed, items were thrown around, but it is impossible to know if anything else was taken. That's because no one knows what Rayburn had here in the first place.

Of course these rooms now look nothing like they did in the discovery photographs. But those photographs make it look like the perpetrator spent a lot of time here.

When I mention this to Laurie, she says, "I can't imagine that Rayburn watched the person ransack the place without doing anything. So the robbery, or the attempt to make it look like a robbery, must have happened when he was already dead."

"Cold-blooded."

She nods. "Very much so. Also seems like it was all planned. Hard to imagine that someone killed him in a sudden burst of violence and then had the presence of mind to set the whole thing up as a robbery."

"Unless it was also a robbery. It might not have been a setup at all; maybe Rayburn had something that the killer wanted. And I don't mean a Rolex."

"You think it was something related to his work?"

"Yes. Or at least a strong maybe."

"Then why smash his computer?" she asks.

I shrug. "That's one of many good questions."

We leave the house with a feeling similar to the one we usually have when we do this. We feel like we learned a lot, when actually we haven't learned anything.

There's an anticlimactic quality to Christmas Eve and Christmas Day at our house, or at least that's my view.

Since in Laurie's version of the holiday season Christmas has been going on for almost two months, there isn't much that changes when the actual day arrives. The tree doesn't change, the music is certainly the same, and the lights Laurie puts up outside and inside the house are still blinking so incessantly it feels like we live on the Vegas Strip. A couple of times I've gone looking for the casino.

Of course, one difference is that there are presents. Laurie picks out the gifts for Ricky, and she always seems to get the right things. She lumps them into three groups: enjoyment, worthwhile, and experiential. The enjoyment part usually involves technology, video games and the like. Worthwhile is most often books, and Ricky is a fairly avid reader.

Experiential was covered this year with the trip to the Adirondacks, and Broadway show tickets for late February. We're all going to see *Hamilton,* which Laurie and I have already seen and enjoyed. Whether the case impacts my ability to take the time for a night out remains to be seen.

I always get Laurie a piece of jewelry from a friend who has a store in Teaneck. I have no taste in jewelry at all, so I'm really just buying it as a placeholder, and I tell Laurie she can return it and get whatever she wants.

She always claims that she loves it, but I suspect she usually does go and return it. She's sure that I will never notice, and she's right. I don't have the vaguest idea what jewelry she wears or doesn't wear; I just don't pay attention.

Laurie always asks me what I want from her and Ricky, and I tell her shirts and chocolate-covered cherries. So she gets me the shirts and also gets me so many chocolate-covered cherries that when I eat them, I can't fit into the shirts.

We don't actually open our presents until Christmas morning, but the dogs get theirs tonight. They receive toys, biscuits, and chewies, and the evening is always so exciting that Sebastian stays awake for about 5 percent of it. He sucks down some biscuits and then dozes off.

We always spend Christmas Eve at home, like we're doing tonight, and Ricky gets to pick the menu. I promise him an extra video game if he chooses pizza, and I'm pleased to say that I have a son who can be bought.

Christmas Day, which for me is usually filled with televised sports, unfortunately has a work shadow hovering over it today. It's a shame, because not only are there five great NBA games on, but the NFL has now decided to play three games as well.

I go down to the jail to see BJ and wish him a merry Christmas. I'm not surprised to find that Doris is already there to spend time with her son, and since prisoners are only allowed one visitor at a time, I wait for her to leave.

By the time I get in, BJ is chomping down on the muffins and cookies she has brought him. All of them have Christmas decorations, which I'm sure does nothing to negatively impact the taste.

It takes all of my willpower not to grab a couple when he offers, but I decline. It feels like I should leave them all for him, even though I really don't want to.

BJ seems in surprisingly good spirits, much better than I would be in similar circumstances. I know he wants to press me on how the case is going, but I think by now he must realize that I'm going to be noncommittal about it.

I head home and settle in the den with the case documents. I keep the games on in the background, almost loud enough to drown out the Christmas music. When the two competing noises mingle, it almost sounds like Troy Aikman is singing that my days should be merry and bright. It's not the best way to concentrate on discovery documents.

The police have done little investigating into Rayburn's life and contacts. They clearly have decided that his only role in this was to be the victim; if BJ killed him, then whoever he associated with in the past is not relevant. He could have been a mob hit man on the side and it wouldn't matter.

But it matters to us because we are going to try to point to an alternative killer. Not surprisingly, there is no "alternative killer" section in the discovery.

But the actual work I'm doing today is not the problem

for me. What hangs over everything is the mountain that a murder case demands we climb.

And it's not nearly just about the work; it's the intensity and the stakes. The future of a young man with his entire life ahead of him, a young man we hope and probably believe is innocent, is depending on me and our team.

We cannot let him down.

That is pressure.

Dr. Jessica Kauffman is the head of the computer science department at Rutgers.

I was surprised she was on campus and willing to talk to me over the holiday, but she didn't resist at all when I called. The Andy Carpenter charm must be even more powerful than I realized; I need to harness and use it for the good of society.

It snowed a bit during the night, and probably an inch or two has stuck. It makes the campus seem even more empty than it is, but probably even more beautiful.

I went to NYU in Greenwich Village, as inner-city as it gets, and I loved that aspect of it. But there is also something nice about this kind of open-air environment. If I'd thrown a Frisbee at NYU back then, I'd have hit a bus, or a mugger.

There is no receptionist at the entrance desk, which is okay because Dr. Kauffman told me to come right up to her second-floor office. I take the stairs, probably my first and last attempt to work off some of the chocolate-covered cherries. There are fourteen steps, one for every thirty-five cherries, though that's just a rough estimate.

The sign at the top of the steps tells me what number

office to go to. When I get there, the door is open. I walk into what is probably her admin's area and I call out, "Hello."

An office door opens and Dr. Kauffman comes out. She's younger, maybe late thirties, and more attractive than I think college professors generally are. At least that's how I remember them.

She confirms that it's me and invites me back into her office. She tells me she has only flavored water to offer me, and I decline. I don't need to have more nonfattening stuff; I just took the stairs to get here.

"So you are now representing Brian?" she asks, once we're settled in. "He always seemed like such a nice young man. This is so awful; I sincerely hope he is not responsible."

"He didn't do it, but I'm not really here to talk about him."

"Oh?"

"I'd rather talk about Professor Rayburn."

She shakes her head, sadly. "A brilliant and incredibly accomplished man at such a young age. No telling what he could have done in the future if he had the opportunity."

"He was a visiting professor?"

"Yes. From Georgetown."

"How does that happen? Why switch schools temporarily like that?"

"That varies. In Professor Rayburn's case, he was collaborating with another professor, Samuel Mullens, who is tenured here. I believe Professor Rayburn just found it easier to be at the same location. Plus, he was said to be a lover of opera, so the fact that we are close to the city and therefore the Met was probably very appealing to him."

"So he taught a full complement of classes?"

"Oh, no. Just one each semester. His function was almost exclusively as a researcher."

"What does Rutgers get out of that? By that I mean, if he's not teaching, how does it benefit the school to have him here?"

"Well, not speaking specifically to this case, but beyond the obvious prestige, the school often shares in the funding that the researcher gets to do his work. The school provides the laboratories, the machinery, and the support and can benefit financially. It's a win-win, for the researcher, the school, and most often for science and society."

"So BJ was in that one class he taught?"

"Yes. It was Finite Element Methods for Partial Differential Equations."

"Sounds fascinating."

She smiles. "It's an acquired taste."

"Did you personally recruit Professor Rayburn?"

She smiles. "He recruited us. He said he wanted to come here, and we said, 'Anytime.' It was a coup to get him. But it was a horrible outcome."

"Do you know much about his life outside of his work?"

She shakes her head. "I do not. I don't believe he had any immediate family beyond a brother somewhere on the West Coast; that is where his possessions were sent.

"He never spoke about his private life to me; nor would I have expected him to. I do know he wasn't married. He seemed fairly reclusive; certainly he did not attend any of the social functions of the department or university."

"Were you aware that he was using recreational drugs?"

She flashes anger. "Certainly not. And I hope you are not going to slander him."

"I'm just reporting the facts; I have no interest in slandering anyone. The drugs were found in his blood; it's in the autopsy report."

"I had no idea," she says, backing off.

"Do you know anyone he was close to here, other than Professor Mullens?"

"I do not, but that is not surprising. I am here if people in the department need me or have a problem, but I do not intrude on their private time."

"Were you aware of an argument that Professor Rayburn had with BJ?"

"BJ?"

"Brian Bremer. His nickname is BJ."

"Oh. I was not aware of it at the time, but have since heard about it. Apparently it did not raise any concerns when it happened. Although . . ."

She pauses, so I prompt her with "Yes?"

"Although in our last meeting he asked me for our handbook showing the procedure for student administrative discipline."

This is a really bad development. If Rayburn told BJ that he was bringing him up on some kind of charges, it substantially increases motive. "Does it surprise you that Professor Rayburn invited Brian to his house to discuss the matter?" I ask.

She looks surprised. "He did?"

"Yes."

"That surprises me a great deal. It goes against department policy; all such matters are to be addressed on campus. Are you sure about this?"

"I am," I say, even though I'm not. All I have so far is BJ's word for that; I haven't seen any proof.

"Strange. The policy is clearly enunciated; I would certainly think Professor Rayburn would have been aware of it."

"Maybe he was and chose to ignore it."

She nods her assent at the possibility. "There's one other thing which might help explain it. I don't see any harm in mentioning it now."

"And that is?"

"Two days before his death, Professor Rayburn came to me and told me he was leaving. I asked why, and whether there was anything I could do to change his mind, but all he would say was 'it's time' and that 'my work is done.'"

"Was he going back to Georgetown?"

"He didn't say. But maybe he was willing to violate the policy because he was leaving anyway."

Dr. Kauffman has nothing else to say that's enlightening, so as I'm about to leave, my curiosity causes me to ask, "What are you going to do with the house Professor Rayburn was living in?"

She smiles. "Make an offer."

I still have little to go on, and I'm not expecting that will change with my meeting this afternoon.

I'm heading to see the prosecutor assigned to the case, Timothy Nabers, at his invitation. I decided to accept, rather than just deal with him on the phone, because I want to get a sense of him before we go at it in court.

I also want to get a feel for how he will come across to the jury. I'm hoping he drools and babbles a lot, but that's unlikely to be the case.

On the way to his office, I call Corey Douglas. "How'd you like to go on a little trip to Washington, D.C.? You seem like the patriotic type; you can visit the Liberty Bell while you're there."

"The Liberty Bell is in Philadelphia."

"Then you can see it on the way."

"What's this about?"

"Rayburn was a visiting computer science professor at Rutgers. His home base, and his life, was at Georgetown. Maybe you can check around down there and find something we can use."

"No problem. Dani's out of town for work, so the timing is perfect."

Dani Kendall is Corey's girlfriend. She's an event planner, and often those events are in exotic places, which causes her to travel a lot. I'm sure Corey will take Simon Garfunkel with him down to D.C.; Corey is to Simon as I am to Tara, and that is saying a great deal.

"There were drugs in Rayburn's system when he was killed; it's an area to explore," I say. "He was getting them from someone. Also, apparently he had decided to leave Rutgers; I'd like to know if he was going back to Georgetown."

"I'm on it," Corey says.

When I arrive at Nabers's office, two things are immediately obvious. They spend a lot more money on office furniture than the prosecution does in Passaic County. They also have absolutely delicious coffee, which I find out when the receptionist brings me some. She volunteers that it's hazelnut cream.

"It's fantastic," I say.

She smiles. "Tell me about it."

Since I just told her about it, there's no reason to tell her again. Within five minutes, Nabers comes out to greet me with a handshake and a fake prosecutor smile. "So you're the famous Andy Carpenter."

"I already knew that."

"Come on back."

We go back to his office, and when we get there, he says, "I see you've already got your coffee."

I nod. "Hazelnut cream. It's unbelievable, like drinking dessert."

He seems uninterested in chatting about coffee, so he

says, "I've been looking over some of your cases. You're a good lawyer."

"Aw, shucks. Enough about me."

"Look, you don't know me, Andy, but I can be pretty blunt. So let me ask you straight out. . . . Why the hell did you take this case?"

"I swoop in and right wrongs wherever I see them. I'm like a legal superhero. In Passaic County they call me Justice Man."

"You think we're dealing with an injustice here?"

"Yup. My legal advice is that you should drop the charges."

He doesn't seem inclined to act on my suggestion. "Bremer's previous lawyer turned down a plea deal."

"No, his client did. Now known as my client."

"Might the change in attorneys have any effect on his point of view?"

"I would say there is zero chance of that."

"So that refusal stands?"

"Stands tall," I say. "No sense pleading guilty to a crime he didn't commit."

"He was found at the scene and then had the stolen merchandise in his possession."

"In the hands of a non-superhero attorney, that might be problematic."

"Come on, you know better than that; you're a smart guy."

"'Everybody in this room is smart . . . and Teresa Perrone is dead. Who do I see about that?'"

"What the hell are you talking about?"

"It's a Paul Newman line from *Absence of Malice* . . . great movie. For the purpose of this conversation, I am Newman and you are Wilford Brimley."

He has a puzzled look on his face, which is appropriate. "Okay. I guess there's not much more for us to talk about. You got everything you need? All the discovery turned over to you?"

"Yup. But while I have you, let me ask you a question. You think there is hazelnut cream in the actual coffee beans, or do they throw some in with the beans and mix it all up?"

"I have no idea."

"I guess it doesn't matter. I don't have to make the stuff; I just have to drink it. But if you find out, you can tell me at the trial."

"So I checked out James Howarth," Sam says.

He's calling at 10:45 P.M., which he probably wouldn't do if he hadn't learned something important. He didn't wake us; I'm in bed watching a football game with the sound off, and Laurie is reading a new book by her favorite author, David Rosenfelt. I don't get it; I tried reading one and it was like sucking sawdust through a straw.

"And? What did you find out?"

"He is not a candidate for attorney of the year."

"What do you mean?"

"He's always scrounging for cases; if he's chasing ambulances, he's not catching them. Mostly handles very small-time drug cases. He seems to have an arrangement with a local bail bondsman; I suspect the guy steers people to Howarth and gets money kicked back to him. But we're talking small dollars."

So far I haven't heard anything to justify a late-night call, but Sam tends to save the good stuff for last. "Anything else, Sam?"

"Yeah, and you're going to like it."

"First I want to hear it."

"I looked into his bank account; I figured you'd be okay with that."

Sam knows two things. One, that entering Howarth's banking records is illegal, and two, that I'd be okay with it.

"What did you find?"

"For the last three years, he's never had more than eleven thousand dollars there, and usually less than two. He's used his overdraft six times."

"So?"

"So in the last six weeks he's made three cash deposits of eight thousand, eight thousand seven hundred, and nine thousand."

"And no idea where it came from?"

"No, all cash, could have come from anywhere. But the deposits were under ten thousand each, which means the bank did not have to report them to the IRS."

"This is very significant, Sam. Excellent work. Of course, that leads into more work. Can you get his phone number? Office and cell?"

"Of course."

"I figured you could. I was in his office on Monday and I left at maybe a quarter to twelve in the morning. I want to know who he might have called after I left."

"No problem," Sam says.

"In fact, let's get his phone records starting three weeks before the murder. But I'm most interested in the time after I left his office; let me know that as soon as you have it."

"Also no problem." Then, "What else is going on?"

"What else is going on? Are we in the chitchat portion of this conversation?"

"I guess so, yeah. Did you watch the Knicks game tonight?"

"Good night, Sam."

"Good night."

When I get off the phone, I tell Laurie what Sam said about Howarth.

"So at the same time that he takes a case for no apparent reason, he gets a sudden large influx of cash from someone other than his new client," she says.

"That pretty much sums it up. And you can add to it the fact that he was clearly pushing BJ towards taking a plea deal, thereby avoiding a trial. I would also say it's a safe bet that he has not done any intense investigating to prove BJ's innocence."

"So how do we read this?"

"Let's examine it from the most benign, and probably ridiculous, point of view. Let's say there is some unknown wealthy benefactor out there who truly believes in BJ's innocence and is willing to spend money to prove it, while remaining anonymous."

"Come on, Andy."

"I said it was ridiculous, but if that were true, then the lawyer who the benefactor hired would not be coaxing BJ to take a plea deal. He would be breaking his ass to find evidence to clear him and fulfill his mission."

"Right."

"So now that we've got that out of the way, we have to assume that the benefactor wants this to go away and not be investigated, and definitely not go to trial. He, or she, has something to lose if the truth comes out."

"Which means that he, or she, either is the real killer or knows who is."

"Correct again." Then, "Tomorrow's another day. Can I turn out the lights?"

"I just want to read a few more pages. I love this guy."

I'm feeling a little better about our situation.

Actually, it would be more accurate to say that I'm feeling better about our client. The situation is still nowhere; we have not found a usable piece of anything close to exculpatory evidence. Of course, we've barely started, so that in itself isn't surprising or too worrisome.

But I'm feeling better about BJ's role, or lack of role, in the events that put him in jail. Someone out there, someone with money, wants him quietly put away for a long time. I see that as a positive for us. If that person really believed in BJ's innocence, he or she would have no reason to opt for anonymity.

Another interesting fact is that Rayburn seemed to make a sudden and unexpected decision to leave Rutgers prematurely. I don't have any idea why that was the case, but it sure as hell wasn't that he was worried about BJ hitting him over the head with a statue.

For now I'm back at Rutgers to meet with the administrative clerk for the computer science department. He's the one who BJ said called him to convey the message that Rayburn wanted to meet with him at his house.

I want to know if Rayburn said anything else to the

clerk about it, or if Rayburn was acting strangely in any way. I also want to know why the clerk was willing to pass on the invitation, since his boss told me it was strictly against protocol for a meeting to have taken place off campus.

The clerk's name is Evan Morris, and he cleared talking to me with Dr. Kauffman. We're meeting in a lounge in the department building, which fortunately is empty when I arrive. I don't like strangers overhearing my interviews with possible witnesses.

Mr. Morris comes in about two minutes after I arrive. He's in his early sixties, which comes as a surprise to me. Since his boss looked to be in her thirties, I guess I just assumed the clerk would be younger. That's probably an example of some kind of ism that I should be ashamed of.

"Hello, Mr. Carpenter," he says, a little formally. I'm not sure if he's nervous because of the situation, or just distrustful of someone who is defending a person who he thinks killed a member of his department.

"Hello, Mr. Morris. Thanks for meeting with me. I won't take much of your time."

"What would you like to know?"

"When Professor Rayburn asked you to call Brian, what did he—"

Mr. Morris interrupts, "I don't understand. Professor Rayburn never asked me to call anyone."

"You didn't call Brian to tell him that the professor wanted to meet with him at his house?"

"Certainly not. That's not how we do things on this campus."

"So you never made such a call? You didn't know that Brian was going to his house that night?"

"As I've said, I made no such call, nor would I have if requested."

"You are the administrative clerk in the department?"

"Yes."

"Could anyone else have made that call on your behalf?"

"There's no one else who could have done so. We are a small department; I don't have people working for me."

"Well, then, I'm going to take even less of your time than I thought. Thank you for seeing me."

I leave and head for the jail. BJ had told me that the administrative clerk for the department had called him, but he hadn't mentioned the name of the person.

As soon as BJ is brought back into the room, I ask him for that name.

"I think he said his name was Morris. I don't know his first name."

"Are you sure it was him? Did you recognize his voice?"

"I don't think I ever heard his voice before. So I'm not sure it was him, but that's what he said."

"He just told me he never called you."

"What? Well, someone did, and they used his name."

"How did you know where Rayburn lived?"

"He told me. He said to be there at eight sharp, that the professor insisted on promptness. It made sense to me because if a student showed up late for one of his classes, he got really pissed off."

I leave with something else to think about. If BJ is telling the truth, and I'm increasingly believing that he is, then he was not just in the wrong place at the wrong time. He did not just happen to be there around the time of the murder, therefore becoming a good person to pin it on.

He was sent to the murder scene for just that purpose. The time and place of the murder were already set, and BJ came in on cue, just like he was supposed to. And the murderer had already left there and gone directly to BJ's house to plant the Rolex and the cash.

Laurie calls me to say that Corey is on the way back from Washington with what he describes as interesting information. He'll be back tonight and come straight to the house to share it. She also mentions that Sam is coming over as well; he's traced Howarth's phone records.

I tell her to ask Marcus to be there also, in case we need him to look into anything that Sam or Corey says.

My last stop before I head home is to see Doris Bremer. There's no purpose to it other than to let her know that someone cares about her son. If I get one of those blueberry muffins in the process, so be it.

She and Murphy greet me at the door; she's smiling and his tail is wagging. She invites me in and tells me how happy she is that I am helping BJ. "We didn't even know you were a lawyer."

"I don't spread it around."

"Well, I am so grateful. I just know you'll bring my BJ home."

"I'll do my best." Then I ask, pathetically, "What's that I smell? Are you baking muffins again?"

"No, but I have some. Would you like one?"

"Might as well, as long as I'm here."

She goes into the kitchen and comes out with a bag that she hands to me. "I put in some extra in case you get hungry later."

"Thank you. Lawyering can make a man very hungry."

I look in the bag when I get in the car and see that there are four muffins for me to take home. Since our family consists of three people, there is likely going to be anger and bitterness when I have to distribute the muffins inequitably.

In my sincere desire to keep my family together and unified, there's only one thing I can do. I suck down one of the muffins on the way home. Now everyone can get one muffin each and not feel slighted, and we can all be happy.

I'm a family-first kind of guy.

Rayburn had not had an easy time of it," Corey says. "He lost his wife a little over four years ago to cancer, and the people who knew him best say that he withdrew from everyone and threw himself into his work. He had always been work focused, but that increased dramatically.

"There is also a widespread belief that soon after his wife's death he began taking drugs and acting erratically. Yet by all accounts he was able to maintain his production at work."

"Where was he getting the drugs?" Laurie asks.

"I don't know that yet, but it was eating into him financially, that's for sure. He was constantly late on his rent, and he sold his car. He was able to walk to campus, so that wasn't that big a problem."

I turn to Sam. "Sam, please check into his finances."

"Will do."

"Do you know why he left Georgetown and went to Rutgers?"

Corey shakes his head. "No, other than it was work-related."

"What was he working on?"

"Some kind of program to detect computer viruses is all I know. The people I spoke with had little understanding of that stuff, and I'm the same way."

"And why was he leaving Rutgers and going back to Georgetown?"

"He wasn't going back to Georgetown," Corey says. "Or if he was, the department wasn't aware of it. I spoke to the dean; he said they had had no contact with Rayburn since he left."

"Sam, check through his phone records. See if he had any contact with other universities, someplace he might have been headed to next."

Sam agrees to do so, and I turn back to Corey. "The drug connection is most interesting to me, and the lack of money makes it more so. If he got in too deep and couldn't pay, his dealer could be a person we could point to as a possible alternative killer."

Corey nods. "I have a lot of feelers out, and I'll make contact with some drug cops down there and see what I can learn."

"There's something else which might tie into this," Sam says. "Every Thursday night Rayburn had an Uber pick him up for a round-trip ride to Newark. It doesn't say how long he was there, but the round trips were always under two hours."

"It's about a forty-five-minute ride from New Brunswick to Newark," Corey says. "So that would mean less than a half hour in Newark."

Sam says he has the address Rayburn was going to, so I ask Marcus to follow up on it.

"Also, Sam, BJ says he got a call from the administrative clerk at Rutgers asking him to be at Rayburn's that night, but the clerk says he never made the call. Can you see if there's a record of it? On BJ's phone?"

"Sure."

"Okay, what have you got for us?"

"I have Howarth's phone records," Sam says. "I still have to go through them carefully. But he made a phone call soon after you left him."

"To who?"

"A guy named Gregori Borodin."

"What kind of name is that?"

"I think Russian," Sam says. "I'll check into him further to confirm. But Howarth made three calls to him in the last two months, and received two in return."

"Do we know anything about Borodin yet?"

"Yes, he's listed as head of security for Thomas Nucci and his companies."

"Who is Thomas Nucci?" I ask.

Corey says, "I can answer that; I've had a few dealings with Mr. Nucci. He's a criminal, you might call him a crime boss that has gone respectable. He's used the money he's earned illegally and built so-called legitimate businesses.

"He owns a bunch of companies, probably all of which do nothing more than launder money. But through it all he's remained a piece of garbage. A dangerous, smart, well-dressed, violent piece of garbage."

"Sounds delightful," Laurie says. "Where does he work out of?"

"If I remember correctly, Elizabeth," Corey says. "But he's not really bound by geography."

"This does not sound like the guy who would be hiring a lowlife like Howarth as his personal attorney. So if we assume that Borodin was acting on Nucci's behalf, we can then further assume that Nucci paid Howarth to represent BJ—"

Laurie interrupts, "Those are big assumptions to make from one Howarth-to-Borodin phone call. He could have dialed a wrong number."

"I know, but we can't hurt ourselves by going there. What we need to find out is what is Nucci's interest in this."

"Any idea how to do that?" she asks.

"None. But I'm going to start with another visit to James Howarth, Esquire."

"You're back," Howarth says when he looks up. He doesn't say it in a way that feels welcoming.

I didn't tell him I was coming, which meant that I risked showing up and having him not be here. I didn't want to take any chances on what might happen if he was expecting the visit; there's no telling what he said to Borodin about me.

"Wow . . . amazing how fast you picked up on that," I say.

"We have nothing to talk about."

"That's disappointing. Just when I thought you were pretty sharp, you show me otherwise. We have plenty to talk about, James. You know . . . lawyer to lawyer."

"I have nothing to do with your case or your client anymore. So you can just turn around and get the hell out of here. You cost me a lot of money."

Instead of doing that, I pull up a chair facing him at his desk. "Funny you bring that up because money is what I want to talk to you about. Who paid you to take on the case?"

"I told you that was none of your business."

"I wasn't really looking for an answer. You know how

we lawyers are never supposed to ask a question we don't already know the answer to? Are you familiar with that? Did they teach that at the Slimeball School of Law? You see, when I asked who paid you, I already knew."

"You trying to fake me out? Trick me into telling you? No chance."

"I've got a hunch you've been faked out a lot in your career, but, no, that's not it. You were paid by Gregori Borodin on behalf of Thomas Nucci."

He doesn't say anything, but the stunned look on his face is a dead giveaway that I'm right. "What I don't know, which is why I'm here, is why they did that. So you can tell me that and I'll be on my way."

"You can go on your way now. I've got nothing to say to you."

I shake my head in fake sadness. "There you go again, disappointing me. You've probably disappointed a lot of people in your time here on earth. But here's the way it's going to play out. You have a choice. You can tell me why Nucci cares one way or another about this case, or you can say nothing. Then—"

He interrupts, "I have nothing to do with Nucci."

"Objection overruled. You didn't let me finish. If you choose nothing, then I will ask the same question of Nucci. And when he wants to know how I found out he's the one who paid you, I'll tell him that you were eager to volunteer the information. I suspect he will not be pleased to hear that."

Howarth looks miserable; he is trapped between a rock and a mobster. Finally, "How did you find out?"

"That's on a need-to-know basis, and I have determined you don't need to know it."

"If I talk to you, do I have your word you will not tell Nucci that we talked?"

"You do. Now hurry up and tell me all about it. Just being in this office makes me want to take a shower."

He looks at me with a significant amount of hatred. "There isn't much to tell. Borodin approached me. He never mentioned Nucci, but I knew who he worked for. Said he wanted me to take the case and promised me a lot of money, with more to come if things worked out."

"In cash."

Howarth nods. "In cash."

"How much?"

"Fifty thousand, with another hundred on the back end."

"And he gave you the fifty?" I already know from the banking records that Howarth's been making cash deposits; I'm asking to see if he's being truthful.

"Yeah, he paid me the fifty."

"And what were your marching orders?"

"To take the case, and to make sure it never went to trial."

"By getting BJ to plead?"

He nods. "Yes. But, hey, I wasn't doing anything wrong. The case is a sure loser; why not try and get the kid a deal?"

"Because he didn't do it. What is Nucci's interest in this?"

"I don't know; I swear. Borodin didn't say anything about that."

Unfortunately, I believe what Howarth is saying. Nucci would have no reason to have his guy confide his motivation to Howarth. Howarth had a specific job to do; he didn't have to know why he was doing it.

"And you didn't really care," I say. "As long as you got your money, you were ready to throw away that young man's life."

"He's a killer."

"We'll find out about that. But one thing we know for sure: you're a piece of shit."

Professor Samuel Mullens can't be more than thirty-five.

Professor Rayburn was also young, as is Jessica Kauffman, the head of the computer science department. Back in the day I always thought of professors as old, but maybe that's because I was a teenager and anyone over thirty seemed like Methuselah.

Mullens agreed to see me when I called, though he seemed reluctant. Rayburn was a colleague and a friend, so I suspect he's not going to be protesting on campus holding up a sign saying FREE BJ BREMER.

We're meeting in his office on campus. His name was on the door, so I am assuming that each professor has his own private office. That means that Rayburn would have had a logical and school-approved place to meet with BJ.

But someone arranged the meeting at Rayburn's house so that BJ could be set up for the murder. At least that's how I am starting to see it.

It's not a good sign that Mullens begins the meeting by telling me he has a class in twenty minutes. We could have started the meeting earlier, but I don't bother pointing that out because I don't want to eat into my twenty minutes.

"So you were a close friend of Professor Rayburn?"

"I was a friend," he says, notably leaving out the word *close.* "I was also a colleague and collaborator."

"How long did you know him?"

Mullens thinks for a few moments. "Maybe four years. We met at a conference; I believe it was in Miami."

"When did you start collaborating?"

"Perhaps two years ago. What does this have to do with his murder?"

"Probably nothing. I collect information and some of it winds up to be relevant, and some not."

"Then your work is not so different than mine." He says this as he looks at his watch, a not-so-subtle message that class time is approaching.

Just then, a young man comes to the door. "Oh, I'm sorry, Professor."

"That's fine, Andrew."

"Here's your keys." Andrew walks in and hands a set of what look like car keys to Mullens.

"Thank you."

"Will you be needing me any more today?"

"No. All good."

When Andrew leaves, I ask, "Your assistant?"

Mullens nods. "The university is good enough to supply each of us with such a person; it's always one of the better students. They expect them to learn something by being around us. It's much like clerking for a Supreme Court justice, minus the prestige."

"So Professor Rayburn would have had a similar situation; that is, a student assigned to help and assist him?"

"That's correct."

"What kind of work were you and Professor Rayburn doing together?"

"That is proprietary information."

"I understand. Did it involve detection of computer viruses?"

He looks surprised, then. "I refer you to my comment about proprietary information."

"Are you aware of any enemies that Professor Rayburn might have had?"

"No."

"What about his drug use? Was that a problem you were aware of?"

Now Mullens looks angry. "Is that what this is about? Impugning the character of a person not here to defend himself?"

The head of the department had a similar reaction; here at Rutgers they are protective of their own. "No, this is about finding the truth wherever it leads."

"Right now it leads to my going to teach my class. Good-bye, Mr. Carpenter."

Mullens gets up and leaves me alone in his office. I could sit behind his desk and find out what it feels like to be an egghead tenured professor, but that doesn't seem like it would be that much fun.

Instead I leave and go back to the main office, where I'm happy to see that the administrative clerk, Evan Morris, is at his post. I ask him if Professor Rayburn had a university-supplied assistant, much in the way that Mullens has Andrew.

He says that Rayburn did and gives me his name, Adam Lusk. It's a positive development in that it gives me someone else to bother.

So many people to annoy . . . so little time.

Marcus Clark figured out where Rayburn was going on his weekly Uber rides, and it wasn't to academic seminars.

As I suspected, it was to replenish his drug supply. Apparently Rayburn wasn't a lucrative enough customer to warrant deliveries, so he had to go to the source.

Marcus is assuming that's what was going on, as he canvassed the neighborhood and found a location two blocks from the Uber drop-off point where they were dealing drugs. It is in a small first-floor apartment with a door out to an alley.

Marcus has pictures of the building and the surrounding area, as well as a plan should we decide that a visit is appropriate. Visiting places like that with Marcus is always a memorable experience, but I like to avoid this when possible, as violence is usually involved.

The drug connection falls into an area that is worth pursuing, but not necessarily to find out who the real killer is. It's more to find a person or persons to point to for the jury to view as a potential killer.

In the real world, drug dealers don't generally want to kill their customers. It's bad for business because if they do, the deceased no longer buy their drugs. Possibly Rayburn owed them money and was refusing or unable to pay, but that is unlikely. He was still making the weekly trips until his death, and he would not have been going there to get drugs if he was seriously in arrears. They would have cut him off before taking drastic action.

And that action would not have been murder. It might have been a beating, or at least a threatened beating. Now it's possible that a beating went further than it was supposed to, but again, I don't buy it in this case. You don't warn someone by smashing them over the head with a metal statue.

But it can work for a jury. The drug world is dangerous and people have no trouble believing that violence and even murder are parts of that world. If we can place Rayburn into it, then in the eyes of that jury he is no longer just a meek, innocent academic. That is true even if he was actually a meek, innocent academic.

Tonight is New Year's Eve, and as eves go, this is my least favorite, although at this point it no longer should be. In my earlier years, I would feel an obligation to go out and attempt to have fun, since the prevailing view among my friends and associates was that only losers stay home on New Year's Eve.

Mercifully, since I met Laurie, things have completely changed, and then Ricky's arrival on the scene cemented that new approach. Laurie's idea of a wonderful evening is to stay home with her family. We have a nice meal and then fail in our first New Year's resolution, which is to stay up to watch the ball drop.

I start the evening by taking Tara and Hunter on a nice long walk through the park. My second resolution is one I can definitely keep: I am going to make sure that nothing bad happens to these dogs, and that we keep walking on into the sunset.

The ground is covered by a couple of inches of snow, yet it doesn't seem to impede the ability of Tara and Hunter to sniff and enjoy the smells. "Happy New Year, guys," I say, and it seems like Tara nods in response. Or maybe not.

I was not planning on working during this holiday, or for that matter during the entire upcoming year. But on some level I am glad that I am.

Without the involvement of our team, BJ was going to spend most of the rest of his life in jail. Howarth was either going to talk him into pleading it out or would have mounted a perfunctory defense that would have resulted in BJ's conviction.

That was Howarth's goal, and he was definitely going to pull it off and collect his money. It is horrifying that he would do that to someone, but if he felt any contrition, it was hard to detect.

My view right now is that Nucci was on some level involved in Rayburn's killing, mainly because I can't see any other reason for him to have hired Howarth. Nucci was intent on burying the case, precluding any serious investigation and sending BJ off to prison.

I don't think Nucci was out to hurt BJ. He was just collateral damage and not someone to worry about one way or the other. Nucci was out to protect himself. From what I hear, he is really good at protecting himself.

Ricky starts dozing off at ten fifteen; then wakes up and heads to bed. At ten thirty Laurie and I ourselves go to sleep. Last year we made it to ten forty-five, so age may be creeping up on us.

I wake up during the night, not so I can check to see if we're approaching midnight, but rather because I suddenly realize that there is something I hadn't thought of.

Something that terrifies me.

I ask for an emergency hearing with Judge Walter Lockett, who is presiding over BJ's case.

It turns out that Judge Lockett is on vacation, so Judge Alice Martinez is assigned to conduct the hearing. She will not be in a good mood, seeing as how this is a holiday, and the prosecutor, Timothy Nabers, will no doubt be equally annoyed.

I'm not thrilled myself to be in a courthouse today, as New Year's Day is filled with great bowl games. But as Hyman Roth so eloquently put it, "This is the business we have chosen."

I tell the judge that it's not necessary to meet in open court, or to have a stenographer present. In point of fact, I don't want a record of it. To get the session in the first place, I also promised that it would not take more than fifteen minutes.

Once we're settled in chambers, the judge and Nabers glare at me in unison. "Why are we here on this, a holiday, when the court is closed, Mr. Carpenter?" she asks.

"I'm sorry for the significant inconvenience, Your Honor, but I believe my client is in serious danger at the jail, and I would strongly request an order that he be put into solitary confinement, with special protections. Any delay could be catastrophic."

"Oh, come on," Nabers says.

"Judge, this will go faster if you could instruct Mr. Nabers not to comment until he has the vaguest idea what he is talking about."

"Mr. Carpenter, I am more concerned with what you are talking about. Please enlighten me on an expedited basis."

I nod. "Understood. And please know that there are things I am about to reveal that I would prefer not to. So I will be careful and hope that the court will accept my declarations at face value without revealing information that could be vital to my case."

"Proceed," she says.

"Thank you. Mr. James Howarth was the attorney for Mr. Bremer until I took over. He showed up at the jail unrequested and volunteered his services; Mr. Bremer had never previously heard of him. He told Mr. Bremer that he had read about his case, believed in his innocence, and wanted to help. None of that was anywhere approaching true."

"Was Mr. Bremer paying for his services?"

"He was not, and did not. Mr. Howarth never even discussed compensation with him. I looked into it, and if Mr. Howarth has a history of pro bono legal work, he has done it well under the radar.

"I have since learned that a third party, who I would prefer not to name, paid Mr. Howarth a substantial amount of money to take the case.

"Even more significant, that person instructed Mr. Howarth to convince Mr. Bremer to accept a plea deal, which he tried and failed to do. Mr. Bremer would not confess to a crime he did not commit.

"Mr. Howarth's further marching orders, should Mr. Bremer maintain his refusal to plead it out, was that should the trial move forward, he was to mount a perfunctory defense, with little or no investigation."

"And you can't name the individual who paid Mr. Howarth?" she asks.

"I would rather not, at least not with Mr. Nabers present; it could jeopardize my case before I have a chance to investigate further. But the individual is known to be dangerous and involved in nefarious activities."

"I'm confused," the judge says. "What does issuing a protective order have to do with the situation?"

"As I said, the person in question had two goals: a plea bargain or a trial which contained no significant defense. Now that Mr. Howarth is no longer in the picture, neither of those goals are within reach. The only way there will not be a trial is if Mr. Bremer is eliminated."

Nabers speaks. "Your Honor, Mr. Carpenter presents no evidence other than his wild theories, which absent evidence he is asking us to take at face value."

The judge turns to me and I say, "Yes, Your Honor, as I said earlier, I am asking you to take everything I said at face value. I am not in the habit of lying to the court, but I would submit that you don't have to judge me as truthful to issue this order. Nor do you have to decide whether my concerns are warranted.

"Simply put, there is no downside to issuing the order, not to the court and not to the prosecution. Mr. Nabers's case is in no way negatively impacted by the type of confinement Mr. Bremer is offered. Also, having him in solitary with special protections does not in any way aid the defense.

"Everything I told you is true. If I admit information about this at trial, Mr. Nabers is obviously free to challenge it. An order of the kind I am requesting does not alter or limit his options one iota. I have no idea why he is opposing it; perhaps he read in the prosecution handbook that whatever the defense asks for, argue against it."

"That's outrageous," Nabers says.

I ignore that. "Now, I am admittedly speculating that Mr. Bremer is in danger in the jail, but it is informed speculation. While there is no damage done to anyone by issuing the order, the risk in not doing so, in my opinion, might well be extremely significant and unfortunately irreversible."

She thinks about it for a few moments. "Very well, I will issue the order immediately. Judge Lockett can review the matter on his return and reverse it if he so chooses.

"Thank you, gentlemen. Enjoy the rest of your holiday."

The conversation with Andy Carpenter had thoroughly unnerved Professor Samuel Mullens.

It's not that Carpenter seemed to know anything that would be dangerous to Mullens. Carpenter did not voice suspicions about Mullens and most notably did not mention Borodin or Nucci.

It seemed to Mullens that Carpenter was simply doing due diligence in defending his client; he was learning as much as he could to help in that defense. Mullens knew it was perfectly predictable that Carpenter would have questions for him; he was after all Rayburn's colleague, collaborator, and friend.

Nevertheless, danger signs were flashing for Mullens. He had googled Carpenter, and he was smart; his reputation was well earned as an outstanding attorney. He would turn over every rock he could find and not stop probing until the end of the case.

Part of Mullens's reaction, or what he himself considered an overreaction, was because he had thought this was all behind him. The Bremer kid was arrested, probably wrongly, but the case against him seemed strong.

Mullens felt some semblance of guilt that Bremer would go to prison despite likely being innocent, but it was not his fault. He knew better, but couldn't prove it even if he came forward. All that would happen would be his own imprisonment or death, and Bremer would probably still be convicted.

Hovering over all of this was Mullens's continued bafflement at the Rayburn murder. Neither Nucci nor Borodin ever admitted to him that they had ordered it, and therefore they obviously had never told him a reason.

It was counterintuitive, unless Rayburn had somehow found out the truth and confronted them. That seemed unlikely, but why else would they have killed him? They needed him, even if they now expected Mullens to come through on his own.

Their confidence in him was misplaced, but there was no way he could tell them that. There was so much he couldn't tell them, including what Rayburn had already accomplished. Mullens was in self-preservation mode; his primary goal at this point was to avoid suffering the same fate as Rayburn.

So he had been going along, one day after another, not knowing what the endgame was going to be. Now, with Carpenter in the picture, there was another player that Mullens could not control, one that posed yet another danger.

Mullens didn't want to talk to either Borodin or Nucci about Carpenter, at least not yet. There would be no telling how they would react, or whether Mullens might get caught up in any violence that might ensue.

Mullens was a scientist, a problem solver by trade.

But if there was a solution to this one, he had better find it soon.

Adam Lusk is the computer science student who had been assigned to help and assist Steven Rayburn. He had the job that Professor Mullens described as being like a Supreme Court clerk. Apparently this is an appointment only given to the top students in the department.

We're meeting in the student lounge, which is again mostly empty because school is still off for vacation. Adam lives near here, so when I reached him, he offered to meet on campus.

He's waiting for me when I arrive and is the first person in this entire case to greet me with a smile. He offers me coffee out of a vending machine, and I make the mistake of trying it. It makes me long for the hazelnut cream days.

He sees the face I make when I take the first sip. "Sorry, I should have warned you. I think that's the stuff they put in carburetors."

"Truly awful. Having it in here is a form of student abuse."

"Maybe you can represent us in a class action." Then, "I just want you to know, I'm a big fan of yours."

"How's that?"

"I almost went to law school so I'm interested in that stuff. I've followed some of your cases. Beyond impressive."

Finally I've run into someone who knows what they're talking about. "You made the right choice. Let's talk about Professor Rayburn."

Lusk nods. "What do you want to know?"

"To start, how bad was his drug habit?"

Lusk looks surprised. "You know about that?" Then, "I guess you do. It wasn't good, but not so bad that he couldn't function. He was still able to perform his work at a very high level. It was hard for me to believe, but he was able to compartmentalize his work and his drug intake."

"What was he working on?"

"I don't think I should go there; you should ask Professor Mullens. They were working together. Even if I wanted to, I couldn't enlighten you very much."

"Was what they were doing near completion?"

"I believe so, but I can't be sure. Professor Rayburn was very secretive about it."

"Why was he leaving Rutgers?"

Lusk looks surprised. "I didn't know he was. Are you sure about that?"

"I am. Was he acting strangely in the days and weeks before he died?"

"He always acted a bit strangely; he was something of an eccentric. I wouldn't say that it increased any."

"Did he date? Any girlfriends?"

"Not that I'm aware of. He could have been gay for all I know. He spent all his time either working or high, but never both."

"No enemies that you know of? No arguments of consequence?"

"No, he was pretty reclusive. He certainly never confided in me about anything. I was supposed to be involved in his work, but he treated me like an errand boy. I considering quitting but thought it would look bad."

"When did you see him last?"

"The day before he died. He wanted me to bring him some papers from his office, which I did."

"Did you know BJ? Brian Bremer?"

"I met him in Professor Rayburn's class. I was a TA . . . teacher's assistant . . . in that class. Seemed like a nice kid, but he and Rayburn didn't get along. They had an argument over a grade; most students wouldn't stand up to him, but Brian did."

"Did it seem like it might get violent?"

"No way. It was no big deal."

"Will you testify to that?"

He hesitates, then, "Of course."

"Did you know that Professor Rayburn asked the department head for a handbook to explain administrative student discipline?"

Lusk looks surprised. "No. Maybe he thought the argument was more serious than I did."

"Did you ever hear the name Gregori Borodin? Maybe Rayburn mentioned it?"

"No, I don't think so."

"What about Thomas Nucci?"

"Sounds familiar, but I'm pretty sure I never heard Professor Rayburn mention him."

I ask Lusk to think about our conversation, and if he comes up with any other relevant information, to contact me. I'm afraid this meeting did not provide much progress, and the coffee was awful. And the worst part is, I set up another meeting for the same location, near the same coffee machine, for ten minutes from now.

Right on time, Mark Abrams comes in. He's a close friend of BJ's who BJ told me will vouch for the fact that his argument with Rayburn in class was nothing of consequence.

"So is BJ going to be okay?" Abrams asks, soon after "hello."

"We'll do our best. You're a computer science student also?"

"For now."

"You're going to switch?"

"Yeah; I just haven't told my parents yet. It's just not for me."

"What is for you?"

He shrugs. "Beats the shit out of me. I'm hoping it will appear."

"You were in the class when BJ and Professor Rayburn had that argument?"

"Yeah, it was nothing."

"You'll testify to that? As well as to BJ's good character?"

"Sure . . . absolutely. I'll also testify that Rayburn was an asshole if that helps."

"It doesn't."

"Well, whatever you need; whatever BJ needs, I'm here."

I don't think I have ever gone this long without going to Charlie's.

Charlie's is a sports bar / restaurant that is quite simply the best place of its kind in the entire world. It is the Tara of sports bar / restaurants—there's no greater praise I could offer.

For as long as I can remember, I've shared a regular table at Charlie's with my friends Pete Stanton, the captain of Homicide for Paterson PD, and Vince Sanders, the ink-and-mustard-stained editor of our local newspaper.

I feel like I've been going to Charlie's for so long that in my mind's eye I can remember heading there after a long day in kindergarten. I used to go almost every night, but then Laurie came along, and then Ricky, and I just wanted to be home more.

But I'm going there tonight, just to get my mind off the case. Also, the national championship game is on, Michigan against Georgia, and I want to see it.

Beyond that, I also have a question for Pete; I want to know if he has ever had dealings with Thomas Nucci. I need to learn what makes Nucci tick.

A number of years ago, Pete and Vince decided that

since I have far more money than they do, I should be picking up the checks. I went along with it, setting up a tab and paying the bill monthly.

Then, when I stopped showing up regularly, they were faced with the unhappy prospect of paying for their own food and beer. Ever resourceful, they came up with a solution: they put the checks on my tab whether I was there or not.

I've continued to pay, though I'm not sure why, and they've continued to stuff themselves at my expense. It works perfectly for everyone involved, with the possible exception of me.

When I arrive tonight, Pete and Vince are already there. Obviously. My seat is empty except for the fact that they have put their coats on it. "Now my seat is a coat holder?" I ask.

Vince shrugs. "They wouldn't let us put the tips for the coat check person on your tab." But he frowns and reluctantly picks up the coats. He and Pete drape them on the backs of their chairs.

"I don't know how you guys don't weigh four hundred pounds with the amount of food and beer you consume. I had to take out a mortgage last month to pay the tab."

"Lucky for you interest rates are low," Pete says.

I don't have to order. The waiter knows that I want a hamburger, burnt french fries, and a light beer, and he will bring them over.

I look up at one of the many TV screens and see that the game is about to start. "Who did you guys bet on?"

"Georgia," Pete says.

"I didn't bet, and now I don't need to," I say. "I'll just root for Michigan."

At the half the score is tied at seventeen. We've mostly been watching the game and only insulting each other during time-outs. Once the teams have left the field, I turn to Pete and ask, "What do you know about Thomas Nucci?"

"He's a lowlife. That's pretty much it."

"That's helpful."

"I know a lot about him," Vince says.

"You do?"

"Well, not exactly. But a reporter who works for me does. She wrote a long exposé on him when she was working for a paper down in Middlesex. But Nucci threatened to sue if they ran it, and the chickenshit editor backed down."

"Have you run it?" I ask.

"No. I would, but we don't have circulation down in Middlesex County, so who would care? But my reporter knows all there is to know about Nucci. Problem is she can't prove a lot of it, so it's tough to print."

"Can you arrange for me to talk to your reporter?"

"I can try, depending on what is in it for me."

"Try real hard, or you'll be trying to find someone else to pay your bar tab."

Marcus Clark and I each have our own lane when it comes to anything dangerous.

I'm the one who decides whether the planned action is worthwhile . . . whether it can lead to a positive result. Once I make that call, then it's up to Marcus, in consultation with Laurie and Corey, to decide how to proceed.

I don't bother giving advice on the mechanics of the operation since I will just be ignored and that will hurt my feelings. The other reason I back off is that I have no good counsel to offer; planning potentially violent confrontations is simply not part of my skill set.

In the case of Rayburn's drug dealer, I've decided that it's time to confront him. It's not that we'll get anything tangible from him; he won't break down and confess. But it might shake things up, especially if Nucci is the ultimate boss of the drug operation.

Doing this at all is a sign of weakness; we have no legal way to implicate Nucci or anyone in his organization in the killing, or to connect him or Borodin to Rayburn. But maybe if we annoy them enough, a path will open up.

Maybe, but probably not.

Marcus spent more than an hour with Laurie and Corey

going over the photographs of the scene, the movements of the principals that Marcus has been observing, and his plan for how we handle it.

I've been going in and out of the room, overhearing some of what they've been saying, but not enough to absorb the whole plan. If they are confident, then I am as well.

Marcus and Corey go in Corey's car, and I drive Laurie in mine. Along the way she fills me in on what is going to happen, and it sounds fine. If we were going to conduct the siege of Leningrad and Marcus was on our side, I would think it sounded fine.

The office or apartment that the drug guys work out of has a door out to an alley. This seems always to be the case; a productive way to fight drug use in this country might be to eliminate all the alleys.

Marcus says that three people are involved, the boss and two others, who act as the muscle to insure no problems arise. Customers arrive between 8:00 and 10:00 P.M., but they don't enter the office. Transactions are done in the alley.

The boss, whose name we do not know, does not come out of the office. He sends one of his colleagues out to provide the drugs and collect the money. The other guy always stays inside with the boss, obviously to provide protection should anyone dispense with the outside guy and try to enter.

Each transaction, according to Marcus, takes less than five minutes. At 10:00 P.M. the customers stop coming, and about twenty minutes later the three men come out, with the boss carrying a briefcase, probably with the day's receipts. But they carefully double-lock the door when they leave, so Marcus thinks that they must keep the remaining drugs in there. They have a car parked in the alley about fifteen feet from the door.

Our group has decided that the logical time to confront them is when they are leaving. That way there will be no customers on the scene to interrupt us, and no need to rush the office.

Laurie, Corey, and I wait about a block away for the operation to start. Marcus has gone ahead to make sure that there is nothing different about their moves tonight, and he will text us when we should join him.

At a couple of minutes after ten we get the text and we're on the move. Corey and Laurie are carrying handguns and I am not; there is absolutely no upside to me having a weapon. Nothing good could come from that; I make Sam look like Wyatt Earp.

Marcus is waiting for us when we arrive. There are no windows out to the alley, and Marcus has determined that there are no cameras. I'm sure the lack of windows is seen by our targets as protection from someone on the outside looking in, but it is actually going to be their undoing. They have no way of knowing that we are out here waiting.

Laurie is standing next to the car that the dealers use to drive off. She is just acting casual, as if she doesn't have a care in the world. Marcus and Corey are to the left and right of the door, each tucked into crevices in the adjacent buildings.

I am down the street, far enough away that the bad

guys will not be able to hear my knees knocking and teeth chattering. I'll be able to see what is happening, but won't approach until I see that things are under control.

After fifteen interminable minutes of waiting, the door opens and two guys come out, followed by the third. I assume the third guy is the boss, and the other two wait as he turns to lock the door. The boss is carrying the briefcase that probably holds the night's receipts.

The locking of the door accomplished, they move toward the car and see Laurie, clearly not what they expected. "Who the hell are you?" one of them says, though I can't tell which one.

She starts to walk toward them, smiling. I can't hear what she says, but it doesn't matter. Marcus and Corey come up on them from behind. Marcus takes the two guys up front, and not surprisingly it's a mismatch.

He elbows the closer guy in the side of the head. The guy falls to the right, banging into his colleague while on the way toward collapsing to the cement. He must be unconscious because he does nothing to cushion his imminent fall.

It takes a moment for the guy on the right to realize what is going on, and I'm not sure he fully does. He throws a punch at Marcus, which has absolutely no chance of landing. Marcus doesn't even bother to block it, he just moves slightly to his left and throws a right into the guy's jaw. He also then falls to his right, much like the first guy did. It's sort of synchronized; they look like unconscious, overweight Rockettes.

Corey, meanwhile, has grabbed the boss and has his arm

around his throat. I hear him say, "If you resist at all, your head will turn to face me but your body won't."

That seems to persuade the guy not to resist. Everybody turns back toward the office and Marcus kicks the door in. It takes one kick and he doesn't even look like he puts that much effort into it; it's as if he's kicking an extra point and not a long field goal.

Corey pushes the boss into the office and Laurie follows. She still has her gun out, but it seems unnecessary. Marcus waits behind, grabs the two large unconscious guys by one foot each and drags them into the office. I'm the last one to enter.

When I get in, I see Corey hand a gun to Laurie. I assume he has taken it off the boss, who is now in a chair and looking a combination of miserable and furious. Corey stands over him, ready to do whatever might become necessary, and Marcus is watching the two unconscious guys, should they make the mistake of waking up.

There's a desk and two chairs in the room, as well as a fairly large safe.

"Tonight go pretty much the way you expected?" I ask, but the boss doesn't answer.

"What's your name?"

"Kiss my ass," he says.

"Actually, that name fits. Okay, Kiss, here's how it's going to go. I'm going to ask you some questions, and you are going to answer them, or your life expectancy will be the length of your average sitcom, minus the commercials. We clear?"

He doesn't answer.

"Marcus, he doesn't seem to understand his role here. I am the questioner and he is the answerer. Can you make him understand that? Maybe by breaking something?"

Marcus takes one step toward him. Having seen how Marcus dispatched his larger bodyguards, Kiss seems to have a change of heart.

"Ask your questions and get the hell out of here," he says, not terribly conciliatory, but I'll take it as a sign of progress.

"Was Steven Rayburn a customer of yours?"

Kiss looks surprised. "The teacher? The guy who got killed? Yeah, for a while."

"Did he pay his bills?"

"That wasn't a problem."

"So why did you have him killed?"

"Come on, man. You trying to pin that on me? You cops? Why the hell would I kill a good customer?"

"Maybe because Borodin told you to."

He does a brief double take, no doubt involuntary. I was just taking a shot in the moment, but it connected. These guys are working for Borodin and therefore Nucci.

"I don't know anyone by that name," Kiss says.

I signal to Corey, and he walks out of the room to make a call. I turn back to Kiss and say, "You're lying, but that's okay. When he bails you out, tell him that you are both going down for the murder of Steven Rayburn."

"Bails me out of what?"

"The Newark cops are on the way here; my friend just called them. My guess is that safe contains a large amount of drugs, enough to put you away for a while. And there's probably a lot of money in that briefcase that you'll never see. Give our best to Borodin."

Corey comes back in, and Laurie and I leave him and Marcus with the three guys. Corey has friends in Newark PD, and he had told them to be ready, so they should be here soon.

We didn't learn much and probably accomplished less, but putting away drug dealers can never be considered a total loss.

We now have two links between Nucci and Rayburn. His security guy, Borodin, is the person who hired Howarth to ineffectively represent BJ in the murder case. He also appears to be the one who was providing drugs for Rayburn through the guys we raided last night.

One possibility that I just thought of this morning was that perhaps Rayburn wasn't even paying for the drugs. When I asked Kiss if Rayburn paid his bills on time, he didn't say "yes." He said, "That wasn't a problem," which could conceivably mean that there were no bills to pay.

What of course I don't know is why Nucci would have wanted Rayburn dead. It couldn't be drug related; in the overall picture of Nucci's businesses, legal and illegal, what Rayburn might have been paying wouldn't even qualify as a rounding error.

Possibly it was related to Rayburn's work, but that also seems unlikely. But even if it is, what could Nucci gain by killing Rayburn? Let's say that Rayburn was doing some work on Nucci's behalf, which I suppose is possible. But why kill him? How could Nucci benefit from that?

Is it remotely possible that Nucci did not want Rayburn killed, that he needed him? Could Rayburn's death have been so damaging to Nucci that he wanted to make sure his killer was punished, so he hired Howarth to make sure that BJ didn't get off?

I strongly doubt that last explanation. Nucci could have let BJ go through the process. There was a strong chance he would be convicted; unfortunately, there still is. But if he somehow got off, Nucci would have other ways of exacting revenge. He could have had BJ killed.

Laurie is focused on a different concern: potential revenge by Nucci and Borodin for what happened last night. "Not only are you investigating the case he wanted under the rug, but you beat up his boys and cost him a lot of money last night," she says.

"I didn't beat up anyone."

"You da boss man."

"I never even told him who we were."

"I suspect they can figure that out," she says.

"Okay, point taken. Let's talk about it later. I've got a meeting."

I've been avoiding it because it is completely foreign to me, but I need to learn what I can about Rayburn's work. I feel a sense of accomplishment when I successfully manage to hit Send on an email, so I know that I will not have a clue about the kind of things Rayburn was doing. But it could be relevant to the case and trial, so I have to enter that world.

Today I'm meeting with Stan Belcher, founder of State of the Art, a software start-up in Teaneck. The meeting was set up by Robby Divine, a friend who has more money than everyone else I know put together, times one hundred. It was not a difficult thing for Robby to arrange, since his equity fund owns 70 percent of the company.

The State of the Art offices are surprisingly conventional, nothing modern about them. That surprises me, but on some level it seems to show a confidence. They obviously have decided they don't have to show how hip they are. I like that; maybe my dump of an office shows the same cool confidence.

Stan and I small talk about Robby briefly. Stan, like everyone else who knows Robby, cannot understand his fanatical obsession with the Chicago Cubs. Robby was born in New Hampshire and has lived his entire adult life in Manhattan, yet he lives and dies with the Cubs.

"So you want to talk about Steven Rayburn?" Stan finally asks.

"I do. Did you know him?"

"I tried to hire him. The guy was a genius."

"Why did he turn you down?"

"Same reason he turned everybody else down. He could have called his shot at any tech company in the country."

"Why didn't he?"

"He was only comfortable in academia, at least that's how I read it. Keep in mind, in that world you are working for yourself, you basically do what you want with much less pressure to monetize what you're doing. And he was surrounded by other eggheads who felt the same way."

"Did he have a particular area of expertise?"

"Not really; he could do it all."

"What about AI?" I ask.

"It's possible, but my guess would be no. That's what everybody else is doing; my sense of him is he would zig when everybody else would zag."

"I had heard that he was working on computer viruses . . . how to defend against them."

Stan shrugs. "Again, could be, but that seems a bit tame for him."

"Do you know Samuel Mullens? He's a professor at Rutgers that Rayburn was apparently collaborating with."

"Sure, I know him. Smart guy, but not in Rayburn's class. Very few people are. Did you talk to Mullens?"

"Yes. He wouldn't tell me what they were working on."

"Why is that important? Could someone have killed him over the work?"

"I'd rather you answer that question."

Stan thinks for a while. Then, "Hard to imagine."

The drug dealer delivered Carpenter's message to Borodin.

He told Borodin about Carpenter's threat to bring him and Borodin down for the murder of Steven Rayburn. Carpenter clearly knew that Rayburn had been buying drugs from him, and that Borodin and Nucci ran the operation.

The dealer had not wanted to go to Borodin; there was always the danger that he would blame him and react violently. But he had no choice; he needed to be bailed out, and Borodin had the money and wherewithal to do it.

Once he was back on the street, he accurately relayed what had happened. Again he had no choice; not only was there the arrest and bust to explain, but there was also the loss of a considerable amount of money and drugs.

The dealer needed Borodin to help him get away; to go back and face the drug charges meant a long prison sentence. With the resources that Borodin had, he could make that happen.

So he met Borodin at the abandoned warehouse where they always met to turn over the cash from the drug sales. That is where he delivered Carpenter's message.

Borodin listened calmly to every word; he was not a

person to overreact, despite his reputation for violence. He had the capacity to analyze situations quickly but thoroughly, to consider all his options before taking whatever steps were necessary.

He did not blame the dealer for what happened; he knew the man had done nothing to attract Carpenter's attention. Carpenter had probably traced Rayburn's past steps, and they led him to the dealer.

The dealer's plea to have Borodin help him get away made sense. Certainly if he did not skip bail, he would be tried and convicted, and there was always the chance that to reduce his sentence the dealer would give up Borodin, and also Nucci.

They could not have that. One way to avoid it would be to help the dealer get away, set him up in some distant city with a new name and identity. Sort of a makeshift drug dealer witness protection program. But there remained the danger that he would be found and brought back to face his sentence.

The other way to do it, with more certainty that he would never rat out Borodin, would be to kill him.

So that's what Borodin did.

I decide to stop at my office before heading home. I want to bring home some case documents, and I also want to drop off my rent check to Sofia Hernandez, who owns the building and the fruit stand on the first floor.

I should have turned up the heat higher the last time I was here because the first thing I notice is that it's really cold. So I turn it up some, but not too far because I'm only going to be here a few minutes.

Suddenly something happens that makes me think that my "few minutes" estimate may be a bit off. The door opens and a man I have never before seen walks in. I have a brief flash of fear that Laurie was right and that this guy was sent by Nucci.

Then I realize the actual person responsible for this guy entering is Marcus Clark. Marcus comes in behind him, pushing him as he does.

I have no idea what the hell is going on, so I ask, "What the hell is going on?"

The intruder says, "Your friend here thinks he captured a bad guy."

I turn to Marcus, and he says, "He was following you."

It's immediately obvious that Laurie went over my head

and had Marcus follow me for protection. When I get home, I will reprimand her severely, or at least I would if I were an entirely different person.

"Why were you following me?"

"To see what you were doing, who you were meeting with."

The guy seems confident and unafraid, even though Marcus is standing behind him. It's somehow disconcerting; I'm always afraid of Marcus, even when we're talking on the phone.

"What's your name?"

"Robert Bridges. Agent Robert Bridges." He reaches into his jacket; Marcus doesn't react so I am assuming he already made sure Bridges was unarmed. What Bridges was reaching for was a badge, showing me that he is an agent of the Department of Homeland Security.

"So, why do you want to know who I am meeting with?"

"That's not something I'm prepared to tell you. But I will say that your actions have the potential to interfere with an investigation we are conducting."

"Into the murder of Steven Rayburn?"

"No."

"Then what do I have to do with it?"

"Next question," he says. "But hurry up, I'll be leaving soon."

"Is this about Thomas Nucci?"

He looks at his watch. "Damn, I have to go."

He's really annoying me, but I've got to go through the motions. "Maybe we can work together. Share information."

"If that opportunity presents itself, I will let you know," he says.

"Good. And then I'll tell you to kiss my ass."

If Bridges is intimidated, he's hiding it well. He just laughs and leaves, but Marcus stays with me.

"Marcus, you don't need to follow me. If I have any problems, I'll call you."

"Laurie said to follow you."

"And I'm saying not to follow me."

"I hear you," he says.

"Are you going to follow me?"

"Yes."

"That's what I figured."

Borodin told Nucci about Carpenter's raid on the drug dealer and the dealer's subsequent arrest and untimely demise.

Carpenter was not a serious danger to them yet, but he showed the potential to become one.

Nucci listened carefully and then asked, "What do you think we should do about him?"

The question reflected an evolving dynamic between the two men. Both realized that Nucci was no longer in full control, but neither openly voiced it. Nucci still had muscle behind him, but Borodin had more. And Borodin had an endless supply of money, while the financial noose around Nucci was ever-tightening.

So they danced around it and pretended that every decision reflected their common consensus. And for the most part that had been true, at least so far.

"We just watch Carpenter," Borodin said. "He can't prove anything, not even close. Killing him would draw way too much attention; it's exactly what we don't want. And another lawyer would just move in."

"And if he gets closer?"

"Then we should reconsider our decision to let him live. When all this is over, he will be dealt with."

Nucci nodded his agreement. "Okay, but it feels like this will never be over. What's happening with Mullens?"

"He's working and says he's getting close. He's a poor imitation of Rayburn."

"He'd better step up, and soon."

That was another thing the two men could agree on.

I hang out in the office for about a half hour, reading through documents but distracted by the visit from Agent Bridges.

He said he wasn't looking into Rayburn's murder, which means nothing either way. He could easily have been lying and probably was.

Actually, he definitely was lying, since there would be no other possible reason for Homeland Security to be interested in me. I would not be on their radar; I've never even applied for TSA pre-check.

He could be interested in Thomas Nucci and probably is. But my only connection to Nucci, tenuous though it is, is in relation to the Rayburn murder. So it all comes back to that.

The question of why he'd be concerned with Rayburn at all is the curious one. It's possible that Rayburn was doing research for the government, something that his department head at Rutgers didn't even know about.

Professor Mullens probably knows; he may have been collaborating with Rayburn on it. But he refused to tell me anything about their work, and Adam Lusk, Rayburn's assistant, claimed not to know anything about it either. He said Rayburn was very secretive, which would make sense if he was working for Homeland Security.

I'm getting ready to leave when the door opens again; this time it's just Marcus.

"There's somebody here to see you."

"Who?"

"A teenage kid. She says she thinks she knows who killed the teacher. She's out in the hall."

"Let her in."

Marcus goes back into the hall and comes back with a young woman. Marcus is probably technically right that she's a teenager, but she might be approaching twenty pretty soon. She can't be more than five foot one, and I doubt any growth spurts are coming.

Marcus looks at me and I motion for him to take a seat. He might as well hear this.

The young woman looks nervous as she says, "Mr. Carpenter?"

"Andy."

"Andy. My name is Sharon Keller. I know you are representing the boy that they think killed Steven."

"You knew Professor Rayburn? Steven?"

"Sort of, yes. It's complicated."

"Have a seat. I have time. I also have water if you want some."

"Please," she says. "I'm a little nervous."

"Don't be." I stand up to get and hand her a bottle of water.

She takes a sip and then says, "Do you know what the metaverse is?"

"I have absolutely no idea, although I think I heard my son mention it once or twice."

"Do you know what avatars are?"

"You mean like the movie?"

"In a way, yes. But there are headsets you can put on, and they take you into another world. Literally, another world. Your avatars represent you there; they are you in another form. But you experience what they experience."

"I think I've seen pictures of those headsets. Those big clunky things, right?" I'm feeling like I'm 112 years old.

"Yes. So people go into this metaverse using these devices, and their avatars interact with other people. I mean, you can do everything there. You can buy land, NFTs, go all over the world, and really do almost anything you can do in real life, but you can do it without leaving your home."

"Okay."

"So I did that. I'm shy, and it was a good experience, at least for a while. I met people and made some friends. One of those friends was Steven."

"He did it also?"

"Oh, yes. He was very much into it. I felt he was like me: a loner who deep down wasn't comfortable with interpersonal experiences, but was trying to overcome that discomfort. I guess you could say we became virtual friends. We'd talk, through our avatars, and it was nice. He was a nice man.

"But there are people on there who aren't so nice. There is stealing and a lot of verbal abuse, and even physical violence. One day I was sexually assaulted by three men. I panicked and couldn't even work the controls to get away. It was horrible."

"You were assaulted online? Not physically?"

"I know it sounds crazy to you, but yes. While it happened online, it felt very physical. It was a nightmare for me; I'm still not over it. I've since read about it happening to other women; in England there's a case where the police are going to charge the men involved." She looks up at me. "I know it must be hard for you to understand."

"I'll take your word for it; I'm sorry it happened."

"I talked about it with Steven; he had seen those men online and helped to intervene to stop it. Steven always gave his real name, but many others didn't. Those men hid behind fake names. But Steven somehow found out who two of them were. He was a genius on the computer; he could do anything. I guess he hacked into their online accounts or something."

"What did he do after that?"

"He warned the men that he was going to go to the police if he ever caught them doing something like that again. They laughed at him."

"Did he go to the police?"

"No, I don't think so. But he did something worse. I don't know all the details, but he infected all their devices with some kind of virus. First he told them what he was going to do and dared them to stop him. They said if he did it, they would come find him."

"Do you know what happened after that?"

"No, I didn't even know until this week that Steven

was killed. When I found out, I knew I had to come see you. I got the first flight I could; I had to wait until I got paid for the week to afford it."

"From where?"

"Denver. I live about an hour outside of the city. When you're in the metaverse, it doesn't matter where you live in real life. You just beam yourself wherever you want to go."

"Do you know where the three men live?"

"Yes; I think I know about the two Steven located, at least generally. One of them said we should meet up in person and said I should come to New Jersey. That they'd show me a good time."

She takes out a sheet of paper and hands it to me. It has two online names, X-er and Shan-man. They are not the most creative at coming up with this stuff. There is a third online name, Ta-al Dude, who is apparently the one that Rayburn didn't uncover.

"Do you think they could have been responsible . . . for Steven?" she asks.

"I don't know; but I'm going to find out. Thank you for doing this."

"Should I go to the police? I just thought that since they have arrested someone, they might not believe me."

"Yes, I think you should file a report with them. But I'd prefer you wait a couple of days."

"I was going to fly home tonight . . . I have a standby ticket."

This is an impressive young woman. She's been through

a traumatic experience, but rather than put it in the rear-view mirror, she's put her life on hold to help someone she doesn't even know.

She would also like revenge on her tormentors, and I can certainly understand that. I'm also going to try to make it happen.

"Can you stay a little while?" I ask. "I need your help. We'll get you a room at a nice hotel, with meals, and I'll pay you well for your time."

"Well, sure."

"And you can cash in your standby ticket. You're sitting in first class on whatever flight home you want."

I call Sam and ask him to come down.

While he's on the way, I make a hotel reservation for Sharon and give them my credit card number for all charges.

Sam gets here within twenty minutes. I introduce him to Sharon and tell them both what I want done. They head off to Sam's office, which is down the hall from mine. He offers to drive her to the hotel when they are finished, so I'm free to go home.

Right now I am thinking of what Sharon has told me as another jury diversion, much like Rayburn's connection to the drug world. If I can credibly establish that the online people that Rayburn was dealing with threatened him with retribution for his infecting their devices, then they become potential killers I can point to. Of course, there is always the chance that they are fourteen-year-old creeps sitting in their mother's basement.

I've asked Sam to check them out so we can decide what to do about them. In the meantime, Sharon is giving Sam a road map to that online world that we can use in the way I want it used.

The technology is well beyond my understanding. I'm

still amazed at things like GPS; that some disembodied voice can direct us to our destination by telling us where to turn. That there are literally other worlds out there that humans inhabit by merely putting on a headset is beyond my comprehension.

And I'm okay with that, which has to be a sign that I'm getting old. Of course, who knows? Someday I might try entering those worlds myself, especially if I find out there are no courtrooms there.

When I get home, I tell Laurie all about my conversation with Sharon. I say that while I know nothing about any of this stuff, her story rang true to me. "I believe it happened just how she said it."

Laurie is more computer literate than I am, but she knows nothing about the metaverse. Trying to describe it to her makes me realize that explaining it to a jury is the stuff of which nightmares are made.

But she knows where Sharon is coming from. "I can see how it could be a traumatizing event. She was watching herself be assaulted; I would imagine the hate and violence could seem incredibly real and certainly personal."

I place calls to Adam Lusk and Professor Mullens and leave messages for them to call me back. Lusk is the first to do so.

"So something has come up," I say. "Did Professor Rayburn ever enter something called the metaverse?"

"Why do you ask?" Lusk sounds wary.

"Because I want to know."

"Sounds like you already know. I'm uncomfortable talking

about him like this. It feels like an invasion of his privacy; I'm not sure he would want me to."

"Do you think he would want us to learn who killed him?"

A pause, then, "Yes, I imagine he would. I suspect the professor spent a good amount of time in the metaverse."

"You saw him do it?"

"No, he was very private about it. But I know he was involved in it."

"How?"

"He had three different headsets that I saw, and once I accidentally walked in on him. I walked out before he knew I was there. It was only a couple of seconds, but I knew what he was doing."

"Do you think he did it for entertainment?"

"I can't say. I'm not sure if he was interested in it as a scientist, or if it was just a pastime, a way to relax, but I would guess he was very involved in it."

"Was that a common practice among his peers? Or among students?"

"I can't speak as to other professors; I doubt that many of them did it, but I have no knowledge of it one way or the other. But many students go there; I'm certain of that."

"What about Professor Mullens?"

"I would be surprised; he's not really the type."

"What about you?"

"Not sure why that's important for you to know, but, no, it never appealed to me, so I never sampled it. I have enough on my plate in the real world."

"Are you aware of any enemies that Rayburn made while doing this?"

"Enemies?" Lusk sounds surprised. "I don't think so. Although it's possible; he was one of the few people who used their real names. But I don't know of any issues he had with anyone."

"Would he have told you if he did?"

"Unlikely; he wasn't into sharing personal things. But I might have been aware of it just by being around so much."

I get off the phone and take the dogs for a walk. The exercise grounds me at a time when I need grounding. I watch them and it's real. This is not a virtual Tara or a virtual Hunter; I can reach out and pet them and it's comforting.

Of course, when they squat and make a "deposit," I would like to hand the plastic bag to an avatar and let him deal with it. But I can't, and that's the price I pay for reality.

It's worth it.

I haven't been visiting my client nearly enough.

I never even got a chance to tell BJ why he's in solitary and being guarded at all times, so that's the first thing he asks me.

"I set it up," I say. "I should have told you; I'm sorry. I was concerned for your safety."

"From other prisoners?"

"Yes. The same people who wanted Howarth to sell you down the river to avoid a trial could attempt other means to avoid it. They very likely have connections within the prison."

BJ nods. "That's a little scary. Make that more than a little scary."

"I know. But we've successfully preempted anything like that now. No one can get to you."

"Great . . . thank you. How is the case going? I know I shouldn't keep asking that, but . . ."

"That's fine, BJ. We're making progress, but a long way to go." It's my standard answer to clients; I don't want them to be either too optimistic or too pessimistic. In this case the answer is probably true as well, although the emphasis should be on *a long way to go.*

"You'll get there," he says. "You've got to get there; this place is no fun."

I don't mention that if he's convicted, the prison he'll go to makes this jail look like Disney World. "Have you ever done that metaverse thing?" I ask.

He laughs. "'Done that metaverse thing'? Sorry, but you sound like my mother when she mentions the 'Google machine.'"

I think he might be implying that I am not hip, when nothing could be further from the truth. I'm as hip as they come.

He continues, "Yes, I tried it a few times. It's not really for me, but a lot of my friends are into it."

"Did you know that Professor Rayburn did it?"

"No, but I'm not surprised. It's state-of-the-art stuff; a guy like that would want to dissect it, study what makes it tick, maybe even improve on it."

"You have everything you need?" I ask, preparing to leave.

He nods. "I'm okay. My mother comes every day; she brings me pictures of Murphy. She told me what happened, how he showed up at your house." Then, with a smile, "He probably knew you were a lawyer. He's a really smart dog."

"Does she bring you any more of those amazing muffins?"

He laughs. "Yeah, and I think she slips some to the guards. Aren't they fantastic?"

"If I grew up in her house, I never would have gone away to school. Any other visitors?"

"Just Mark . . . Abrams. He thinks I want to hear how

much fun everybody's having, partying and that stuff." BJ smiles. "I don't."

I leave the jail and head to a diner in Hackensack to talk to Mariah Covey, the reporter that Vince told me wrote an unpublished story about Thomas Nucci.

She's waiting for me at a table in the back when I arrive and waves to me. At least I assume it's her because she is young and attractive, and I haven't had too much experience in my life with women like that waving to me.

After we make small talk and tell each other to use Mariah and Andy, we order coffee. Then she says, "Vince says I should talk to you to ensure his future nourishment."

I nod. "The last time Vince picked up a check was during the Clinton administration."

She laughs. "He's not too good paying salaries either. But he makes up for his cheapness with a lack of charm and grace."

"True. But when you peel away that veneer of boorishness and dig deep, there's an endless supply of boorishness under there."

She laughs again. "Okay, now that we've agreed on Vince, how can I help you? He tells me you're interested in Thomas Nucci?"

"I am. I want to know whatever you can tell me."

"I know you're representing Brian Bremer; does your interest in Nucci have to do with that?"

"It might."

She smiles. "Sorry, I'm a reporter so I ask questions. Thomas Nucci is Tony Soprano if Tony went to Wharton and flunked out. He thinks he's a savvy businessman, but his businesses have been started and supplemented by drugs, gambling, prostitution, and murder for hire. He's a hood in an Armani suit."

"What kind of legitimate businesses does he own?"

"Fast-food restaurants, a chain of tire stores, a few bowling alleys, convenience stores, a software company . . . anywhere he can launder money."

I interrupt her. "A software company?"

She nods. "Yes. They make games, mostly gambling-oriented. You can play blackjack, roulette, whatever, online. And they do antivirus software. Supposed to block all the stuff that's trying to infiltrate our computers."

"And that company is not doing well?"

"Few of his companies are; he just spreads mismanagement wherever he goes. He hired his cronies for top management positions because he trusts them. Sometimes that trust is warranted, sometimes it isn't. But none of them have any idea how to run a business."

"And his illegal activities?"

"Not doing much better; he's feeling the crunch. Legal gambling has really hurt him, and the Feds are coming down hard on the drug end. But a bigger problem is that he's also been encroached on by ethnic gangs; that's the wave of the future, and the future is here."

"What do you mean?"

"The Russians, Mexicans, even the Chechens have all moved in on Nucci's territory, and they're more ruthless than he is. Nucci has had to make some accommodations, especially financially. He can't pay his people enough to hang on to them in this new world."

"What kind of accommodations?"

"He's in bed with the Russians. He had to pick one, and they're the most rational. Plus they are the best funded."

"So he's in a partnership of sorts?"

"Of sorts. It's hard to know who is calling the shots. But Nucci is not the best bet to wind up on top. He will eventually lose his relevance."

"Do you know a guy named Borodin?"

She smiles, but it's humorless. "Do I ever. He threatened me; he is a very dangerous guy. Make that extremely dangerous."

"And he works for Nucci?"

"Or Nucci works for him. It's an unusual relationship."

"How so?"

"Borodin represents the Russians, which gives him a lot of power. Maybe the ultimate power."

"Let's go back to the software company," I say. "Who runs it?"

"I'd have to check my notes again, but I think Nucci handles that one personally, which is one of the reasons it's so unprofitable."

"He has an expertise in computers?"

She laughs. "No chance. I doubt he can turn one on. He brought in some experts to consult."

"Maybe Steven Rayburn?"

"Not that I know of. But he did bring in another Rutgers professor . . . a guy named Samuel Mullens."

Boom.

Until now, the only evidence I had connecting Borodin and Nucci to BJ's case was James Howarth, and possibly Rayburn's drug dealer.

Nucci and Borodin paid Howarth to represent BJ and effectively bury him, but I hadn't been able to make any progress toward finding out why. My assumption had been, and continues to be, that they either committed the Rayburn murder themselves or were protecting whoever did.

But now Mariah Covey has provided another crucial link. Professor Samuel Mullens consulted, or still consults, for Nucci's software company. He's the same Samuel Mullens that was Steven Rayburn's collaborator.

The other important fact that I got out of my conversation with Covey was the Russian connection to Nucci. This is particularly interesting because of the visit I had from Agent Robert Bridges of Homeland Security.

It makes sense that Homeland would be interested if Russians are involved, particularly if those Russians have a connection to the Russian government. I don't know that it's the case here, but it wouldn't surprise me. They're not getting their funding from flipping burgers.

Of course, I still have no idea why these players would have wanted Rayburn dead. If he was working with them, whether directly or through Mullens, then he would have been valuable to them. Why kill him? Was he threatening to rat them out for something they were doing? Had he decided to quit whatever conspiracy it was, and so they had to silence him?

If there is a weak link in all of this, the most likely one is Mullens. We have to figure out a way to expose him, to get him to panic, and we have to do it quickly. There's no way to know if he was on board with killing Rayburn, or if it represents an example of what could happen to him, thereby keeping him under their control.

I call Sam and ask him to do a deep dive on Mullens, on his phone records and his financials.

Then I call Jessica Kauffman, the head of the computer science department at Rutgers. "Mr. Carpenter, I was going to contact you," she says when she picks up.

"What about?"

"I've asked everyone I could ask, and no one in this department called on behalf of Professor Rayburn to ask Brian to come to his house that night. Or any night."

"Thank you. That tracks with what I've learned."

"So to what do I owe this call?"

"You told me that professors at your school who do a lot of research teach very few classes."

"That's correct."

"And you said that they often get funding to do their work, in which case the university might share in that."

"Also correct."

"Who was funding the work that Professors Rayburn and Mullens were collaborating on?"

She is silent for a few moments. Then, "Sometimes that information is public and sometimes private, so I couldn't always share it with you. In this case, however, there is nothing to share. There was no outside funding that I am aware of."

"And that was okay with the university?"

"They were going to publish some results when they were ready and would then solicit funding. And since Professor Rayburn was a visiting professor, you might say we were more tolerant than we might otherwise be. Besides, there was every likelihood that their work would reflect well on the university."

"Could they have been receiving money without you knowing it?"

"Certainly possible, though it would be disappointing. We expect our professors to behave honorably, but we don't rigorously police them. This is an academic community."

I thank her and get off the call. I have to head down to my office. Sam and Sharon Keller have been working out of there, and Laurie, Corey, and Marcus have joined them as I suggested.

They're ready to update me on their progress. As Sam overdramatically put it when he called to summon me, it's "go time."

Sam brings me up-to-date on where things stand, as Laurie, Sharon, Corey, and Marcus listen.

They obviously already know what he is going to say; I'm an audience of one.

"So as you suggested, Sharon got me into the metaverse in which she was assaulted by the three men," Sam says. "I used my own avatar, but deliberately had very little interaction with them, or at least the two of them that were there. I just observed.

"I believe they were the same two that Rayburn identified and threatened on Sharon's behalf. That was X-er and Shan-man. The third person, Ta-al Dude, is probably a more casual user of this system, and we never ran into him."

"And you're sure you got the right two guys?"

"Definitely," Sharon says. "No question about it."

Sam continues, "So once we identified them, we went online with an avatar for Laurie, using a different name, of course. She established a brief relationship; they didn't do anything terribly wrong . . . just a few wisecracks. Nothing that would have concerned anyone if we didn't already know their history.

"The next day we went online as Laurie, and when we saw they were there, she posed a question about buying a car, asking if anyone knew of a used car for sale. Low mileage, preferably a convertible, under twenty thousand. She said she needed one right away for work as her car had died.

"One of the two guys said he knew of one that a friend had; it fit her description of what she was looking for perfectly. They could get her a good deal on it, only seventeen thousand, but it had to be cash. Of course she jumped for it, and they said that they would deliver it, but she should have the money ready. She told them she needed a couple of days to get the cash."

"Where are they bringing it?" I ask.

"Dani's house," Corey says, referring to his girlfriend. "She's selling it and moving in with me. She's happy to let us use it."

Sam says, "This way if they do some research, they'll find out a single woman lives there, and they won't be suspicious."

"Good call," I say. "I assume we have a plan for when they arrive?"

Sam nods. "We sure do. Laurie?"

Laurie takes me through it. It sounds pretty foolproof; the two guys will certainly regret it if they show up. That is, unless they turn out to be legitimate used-car salesmen.

It's going to happen tomorrow night, and I'm actually looking forward to it. I like Sharon, and at the very least we are going to get revenge on her tormentors.

The best part is I am not going to have to do anything physically. If something like that becomes necessary, I have Marcus, Corey, and Laurie to handle it on my behalf.

You might call them my avatars.

There are a number of possibilities when it comes to Professor Samuel Mullens and his role in this case.

The first is that he is knee-deep in a conspiracy with Nucci and Borodin and participated in, and maybe even committed, the murder of Steven Rayburn.

The second is that he is a participant in that conspiracy but had no idea that Rayburn was going to be killed. He could have been okay with it, or terrified by it, thinking he might be next. Rayburn's killing could even partly have been done as a message to keep Mullens in line.

A third possibility is that Mullens is outside the conspiracy; that he connected Rayburn and Nucci through his consultancy to their software firm, but then had nothing to do with what transpired between them after that. I would say that's the least likely.

But what is definite is that if we are going to penetrate what the hell is going on, the most promising tactic would be to go through Mullens. He has no criminal history that we know of, no living or working in this kind of world. He is far more likely to crumble than Nucci or Borodin.

And even though we actually know little about what is happening, we do know enough to effectively rattle Mullens's cage.

Having rattled a number of cages in my long and semi-glorious career, I have learned that it's most effective when unexpected. There is no sense in giving the rattlee advance knowledge that the rattler, in this case me, is about to strike.

So I show up at Mullens's office unannounced, and he's not there. His assistant, Andrew, tells me that Mullens is teaching a class, which will be over in fifteen minutes, but I can wait and see if he comes back to the office afterward.

So I do, and he does.

"Mr. Carpenter, I wasn't expecting you," Mullens says. "I don't believe you have an appointment?"

"Nope; I took a shot that you'd be here. I have a few more questions to ask you, if that's okay."

"I suppose . . . I don't have a lot of time." He can't use the "I have a class" excuse like last time, since the class just finished, so he doesn't bother to come up with an explanation for his limited availability.

"It won't take long," I say, and I follow him into his office.

He doesn't offer me anything to drink; I'm sure that would take too much time, and he doesn't have a lot of it.

"How long have you been working for Thomas Nucci?" I ask.

He looks surprised definitely, scared maybe. "What kind of a question is that?"

"A direct one. Those are my favorite."

"I barely know him. He is a co-owner of a software company which I sometimes consult for. I'm aware of his reputation, but I really know very little about him. Why do you ask?"

I ignore his question. "What about Gregori Borodin?"

He does his best to look puzzled. "I don't know anyone by that name." I think he's getting worried, but he's smoother than I expected.

"Are you saying you forgot that Nucci and Borodin engineered the murder of Steven Rayburn? I would think that's the kind of thing a professor would remember."

"So you are desperately trying to find someone other than your client to blame for this?"

"I was desperate a while back; now I'm feeling more confident. I've learned a great deal."

"I think this meeting is at an end."

"What is at an end is your time as a free man, Professor. So here's your choice. You either tell me and the authorities what you know, and how you know it, or I am going to bring you down with your pals Nucci and Borodin. You can all play computer games in adjoining cells. But the good news is that you'll be there long enough to gain tenure."

"Good-bye, Mr. Carpenter."

"I'm glad we had this chance to chat," I say as I head for the door. "I think it's made us closer."

As soon as I get to the car, I call Sam, as we planned. "I just left his office. Let me know as soon as you find out if he calls anyone."

"I will. But if he uses the office phone from the school switchboard, it will be tougher."

"I understand. Do what you can. I'll be right over. Are we set up for act two?"

"We are. We're doing it from your office."

I go down there and Sam is waiting for me. "We're using your desk phone," he says, so I go to it. "Anytime you're ready," he adds.

"Hopefully he's in."

I dial the phone, and the person who picks up says, "Howarth."

"This is Andy Carpenter."

"What the hell do you want now?" Clearly he does not consider us buddies.

"I just wanted you to know that I'm going to subpoena you to testify at the Bremer trial."

"What?" The one-word question is his way of expressing outrage, rather than indicating he didn't hear me.

"You heard me. You're going to testify to the fact that Thomas Nucci and Gregori Borodin hired you to represent BJ, with instructions to get him to plead it out. And to make sure he loses at trial if he doesn't plead."

"This is bullshit. You swore you wouldn't tell anyone."

"No, I said I wouldn't tell Nucci. And I haven't. I'm a man of my word."

"There is no way I'm going to testify to this; Nucci would bury me if he finds out I told you."

"That's up to you, but you'll be under oath. Oh . . . there's one other thing I forgot to mention. I'm recording this call."

"You can't do this to me, Carpenter."

"Sure I can. New Jersey is a one-person-consent state for taping calls, so it's completely legal. You're a lawyer; I would have thought you would know that."

Carpenter's visit sent Samuel Mullens into a full panic.

He seemed to know everything, or at least enough to implicate Mullens, Borodin, and Nucci in a conspiracy. That might even include murder, though Mullens had nothing to do with Rayburn's death.

If they were in fact the ones who'd killed Rayburn, Mullens believed, it was a terrible mistake. It focused attention on them and was the reason Carpenter was involved at all. It was even counterproductive; Rayburn's genius was crucial to the operation.

Unlike with the last Carpenter visit, Mullens had no choice but to inform Borodin about it. So he called him and described his entire conversation with Carpenter.

Borodin listened silently until Mullens finished. Then all Borodin said was "Say nothing to anyone. I will get back to you."

"Carpenter is not going to let this drop."

"Say nothing to anyone. I will get back to you."

Click.

We're set up and waiting at Dani's house for the two guys who claim to be selling a used car to Laurie.

Corey, Marcus, Sam, and I will be out of the room when Laurie welcomes them. I just hope they show up; it's always possible that they might sense a trap and think it's not worth the risk.

That turns out not to be a problem; they may be assholes, but they are punctual ones. At the appointed hour of 9:00 P.M. they show up, pulling their car into Dani's driveway. They only have the one car, and it's not a convertible, which is what Laurie was told they were bringing.

I'm watching from a side window as they get out of the car. These are not kids; they're probably in their late twenties. And they are large and intimidating looking; their avatars don't do them justice.

They go to the front door and ring the bell. Laurie lets them in, and I hear her say, "That's not a convertible out there."

"Yeah, that's okay. A friend of ours is following with your car."

"When?"

The same guy, who appears to be the talker of the group, says, "When he gets here. You got the money?"

"I've got it. But I want to see the car first."

"I told you it will be here," the talker says. "Where is the cash?"

"It's not cash. It's a check," Laurie says.

The nontalker makes an exception and says, "This is bullshit."

The talker adds, "What are you trying to pull? It was supposed to be cash."

"I know, but I wasn't comfortable getting all that cash. The check is good, but I don't like this."

Suddenly a knife appears in the talker's hand. "You're going to like this even less."

"What are you doing?" Laurie asks, pretending to be scared. "You need to leave now."

The talker smiles. "If there's no cash, maybe you can pay us another way."

Just as suddenly as he produced a knife, Laurie takes a gun out of her pocket and points it at them. "Or maybe not," she says, smiling.

"What the hell?" the talker says, and as he does, the nontalker makes a break for the front door. He opens it and runs directly into Marcus Clark's elbow. It sends him flying back into the room just as Corey and I enter from the hallway.

The talker turns to either go to the door or attack Marcus, proving that just because he's verbal doesn't mean he's bright. Marcus chops down on the arm holding the knife; I can hear the crunching sound all the way across the room.

Marcus then throws a right that doesn't travel more than a few inches, but that deposits the talker in a heap on top of his silent partner.

Both of them are out cold. They are apparently not as tough when no avatars are involved.

Unconscious people are notoriously hard to question. They just lie there, showing no interest in anything people are saying to them. It's annoying, but they seem not to care. I tell Sam to turn off the video and start a new one; I will probably want to keep them separate.

Even with dumping glasses of water on their faces, it's almost ten minutes until the first one comes to, and the talker follows a couple of minutes after.

If they were in the NFL, they would go into concussion protocol, but they get no such consideration in the tough-ass world of Andy Carpenter. They threatened Laurie with a knife; I am going to see that their lives take a pronounced turn for the worse.

We question them while they are still on the floor; it will make them feel more vulnerable, though I doubt they are in the mood to cause trouble.

"Tell us about Steven Rayburn," I say.

"Who?" the talker says, not a promising start.

"He's the professor who you met online and who hacked into your devices."

"That son of a bitch," the talker says. "He ruined my

computer and two headsets. My computer guy can't figure out what is wrong."

"Can I get his computer?" Sam asks. "I want to take a look at it."

"What's your address?" I ask, and the talker tells me. Then I ask for his house key and he hesitates. Marcus takes a step forward and the talker stops hesitating and gives it to me. I flip it to Sam. I ask where the computer is and the talker tells me it's in the den.

"Is there anyone in your house tonight?"

"No."

"Okay, let's get back to Rayburn. We know you killed him."

"He's dead? That's the best news I heard all day."

"He threatened you, ruined your devices, and you didn't do anything? You just let him slide?"

"He was on our list."

I believe him that they did not kill Rayburn, and even though it doesn't help our case, that wasn't really what tonight was about. It was about getting revenge for Sharon and causing these guys significant pain. We've done both, but it's time to increase the pain.

I signal to Laurie and she calls a cop friend who she had alerted. I then hold up one finger to Sam, indicating that he is to provide the police with only the first tape, the one where the talker threatened Laurie with a knife and came after her.

"Here's the way this is going to go down, losers. The cops are on their way, and you're going to take a big fall for this. Attempted robbery and assault with a deadly weapon. You're going to do hard time, with no avatars to lay it off on.

"If and when you get out, we will be watching you, online and in the real world. And if we see anything that makes us come after you, you will wish you were back in prison."

I turn to Marcus. "After the cops pick up this garbage, can you take Sam to get that computer?"

Marcus nods his agreement, and all that's left is to wait for the cops. They show up, we give them the tape and our statements.

All in all a productive night, though unfortunately not for BJ.

When Mullens got home, Borodin was waiting for him with two other men.

Mullens felt a flash of fear that was almost overpowering. He tried to calm himself by the realization that they could not kill him; they needed him.

On the other hand, they needed Rayburn even more, and he was dead and buried.

"I didn't expect you," Mullens said, unable to conceal his nervousness.

"No one ever does," Borodin said. Then, "Hurry up and pack some things, you're leaving here."

"Where are we going?"

"You'll see when we get there."

"I can't leave; I have responsibilities," Mullens said, weakly.

"Did you get the impression that you had a choice? Now get moving and pack; this is better for everyone. You'll be safer this way."

The logical portion of Mullens's brain was trying to be heard over the fear. Not only did they need him for the completion of the project, but if they were going to kill him, why would they want him to pack his things?

That same logical part of his brain unfortunately answered the question. If he packed things and took them with him, it would appear that he left voluntarily and deliberately went missing.

"Where are we going?" Mullens asked again. It was an empty question; there was no chance that Borodin would tell him the truth, whatever that truth might be.

"That's not your concern. You'll be somewhere where you'll be safe and can work without interruption."

"People will think I ran away."

"People will be right. No more talk; get your things and let's go."

Mullens did as he was told. He had no choice, none at all, and he knew it.

His fate was in Borodin's hands.

There comes a time in every case when the intense investigation phase gives way to trial preparation. We are nearing that time.

That's not to say that the investigation ends; far from it, especially in this case. We have a long way to go before we will be fully prepared to go into court and have a chance to successfully defend our client.

But the bottom line is that we have one task, and one task only, and that is to get the jury to feel that BJ could reasonably be innocent. We obviously don't have to prove that innocence; we just have to create that reasonable doubt.

It sounds a lot easier than it is.

The most important thing we have to do to accomplish our goal is to have a credible theory of the case, which translates to a story to tell. If we are vague on what we think is the truth, then the jury will dismiss us and side with the prosecution, which certainly has a coherent theory.

I believe that Nucci and Borodin had Professor Steven Rayburn killed. I don't know who actually brought the statue down on his head, but for now it doesn't matter. They ordered it.

Professor Samuel Mullens, Rayburn's colleague, collaborator, and friend, was and is part of the conspiracy. Together they were working on some kind of research, financed by Nucci and Borodin, that is the key to the entire case. I don't know what that research is, which is a serious problem for the defense. But I believe it was ultimately designed to greatly benefit the Russians, which explains Homeland Security's interest.

Rayburn at some point went off the reservation; he either wanted out or was threatening to go to the authorities. That got him killed. I have to assume that his death means that Nucci and Borodin believe Mullens is capable of successfully completing the research.

I believe that BJ represented a patsy to frame for the killing. Probably he was chosen because of the argument he had with Rayburn in class; Rayburn may have mentioned the incident to Mullens and somehow it got back to Borodin.

The reason that BJ was framed was to preclude any serious investigation into Rayburn's recent work. If he was just found dead, without an obvious culprit like BJ, then that investigation would have taken place and could have threatened the secret operation.

Nucci and Borodin would not have been terribly worried about being blamed for the killing; I'm sure they've gotten away with such things before. To tie it to them would have been difficult to do. So it was the uncovering of what Rayburn was doing that was the danger to them; once BJ was arrested, that became far less likely.

To make sure that the cops would look no further than

BJ, Howarth was brought in as his attorney. He was an insurance policy to make sure that BJ would be convicted and the case closed.

I'm going to call Howarth as a witness in the defense case. He will have to testify truthfully that Nucci and Borodin hired him because I have the incriminating tape of our phone conversation.

Lying exposes Howarth to a perjury charge, though he might see that as the lesser of two evils rather than infuriating the bad guys. Either way, I suspect the phone tape will be enough to get his name removed from their Christmas party list.

But the overall plan to frame BJ was designed to solve all of their problems, and it almost worked. Murphy the terrier mix messed up their scheme by arriving at my house. Lassie could not have done it any better.

Now I have to justify his confidence in me.

I've spent almost two days in trial preparation, coming up for air only to take Tara and Hunter for walks.

We've gotten quite a bit of snow lately and I suspect Eastside Park will be covered in the white stuff until spring. I don't care much either way, but Tara and Hunter are delighted by it. They pause every once in a while to roll around on their backs, before getting up and moving on. Life is simple for them.

As I often do, I use Tara as a sounding board in my trial prep. I would discuss it with Hunter as well, but while I love him dearly, he just does not possess Tara's fine legal mind.

"Tara, the key is how I portray Professor Rayburn. Juries don't like it when a lawyer trashes the victim, so I can't go overboard doing it, but I can't let him off the hook either."

Tara tilts her head slightly, an adorable way of telling me that I'm not being clear. I wish she could talk; it would make these conversations easier and more productive. But if she could talk, then she wouldn't be a golden retriever, she'd be a person, and that would be unacceptable.

If everyone were a golden retriever, the world would be a better, albeit hairier, place.

"I plan to introduce his drug use; that was in the autopsy report. I can try to tie him to the dealer in Newark, and then tie that guy to Borodin, but it's going to be difficult to do."

No response from Tara at all; I think she's bored with this. She'd rather roll around in the snow.

"The crucial thing will be connecting Rayburn to Nucci and Borodin, whether through drug use or another way. I think I can do that, but it will depend on how accommodating the judge is in letting this stuff in. Nabers will certainly fight me every step of the way.

"Mullens is also very important to the story, and I have a direct connection between him and Nucci via the software company. I think Mullens is a weak link; I still need to get him to crack, even a little bit.

"Tara, if you're not interested in this stuff, just say so. But pissing in the snow while I'm talking about my case is very disrespectful."

She doesn't respond at all, so I'm going to give her the silent treatment and not think about the case out loud. That'll teach her.

Another important witness will be Adam Lusk, Rayburn's assistant and TA in his class. Lusk can speak to the drug use and to Rayburn's erratic behavior. He can also attest to the tremendous secrecy with which Rayburn guarded his work.

There is nothing illegal about that secrecy, but I can

make it sound suspicious. In fact, it probably is suspicious. Lusk was supposed to be his right hand; Mullens likened the job to that of a Supreme Court clerk. Lusk should have been included in whatever Rayburn was doing.

I have to do all this without obviously and overtly trashing Rayburn. Most important is that I show that, innocently or not, he was involved with people who are potential killers. It's not going to be easy.

When I get back from our walk, Laurie comes out on the porch to meet me. She hasn't put a coat on, so I suspect that whatever she has to say is important, and she wants me to hear it right away.

"Corey just called. Professor Mullens is missing."

"What does that mean?"

"Mullens didn't show up for class the last two days and then missed a mandatory faculty meeting. He wasn't answering his phone, so they sent the police to his house. He's gone; it appears he packed some things and left."

"So the police are involved?"

"Yes, they were notified this morning. Corey said that while they don't suspect foul play yet, it's significant that Mullens's car is still at his house. Either he had help in leaving voluntarily, or he had no choice. But you don't run away in an Uber."

"He didn't leave voluntarily," I say. "He must have told Nucci and Borodin about my visit, and they removed him from the picture."

"You think he's dead?"

"Not sure. See if you can find out if his computer is

gone. If they still need him, then they'd keep him alive and working until they get what they want. If they've already gotten it, then he's history."

"And what does this do to the case?"

"If he's not found alive, it's a major setback. Mullens knows everything; he's knee-deep in the operation. We need him to tell us and the jury what the hell is going on."

James Howarth had gone over his conversation with Andy Carpenter at least a hundred times.

He needed to remember the exact words he'd said to Carpenter, but he just wasn't able to replay them accurately in his mind. Had he confessed to the relationship with Borodin and the reason he represented Bremer or had he just not disputed it?

Everything depended on it. If he obviously implicated himself on that call, then he could not go on the witness stand and deny it. The tape would contradict him. It would be the worst of both worlds: he'd be liable to a perjury charge and violent retribution by Borodin.

If his words were vague and subject to interpretation, then he could deny everything and get away with it. Had he left himself any wiggle room?

The problem was he just could not recall his exact words, and he had no way of finding out what was on that tape. He wouldn't learn what he actually said until Carpenter played it in court, and then it would be too late.

He made what he thought was the logical decision. He would assume that the tape was vague enough to provide him some room to maneuver, because if it was otherwise, he was a dead man anyway. In fact, spending time in jail for perjury might be the only way to escape Borodin's wrath.

But this could not come as a total surprise to Borodin; Howarth had to get ahead of it and warn him of Carpenter's suspicions. Howarth wouldn't mention the tape, but he would say that Carpenter had found out independently that Borodin hired Howarth. That much was actually true, though Howarth had no idea how Carpenter had found out.

So Howarth called Borodin. It was the first time they had spoken since Carpenter took over the case. At that time Carpenter had not yet mentioned Nucci or Borodin, so Howarth hadn't said anything about it. He had just said that Carpenter was a friend of Bremer's and had been hired.

Borodin seemed to have taken the news in stride, but Howarth had no way of knowing what he was thinking.

The conversation this time was brief and otherwise uneventful. Howarth got off thinking he was fine for the moment, pending the potential playing of the tape during the trial.

That would be a disaster . . . or not. Howarth simply could not remember. He wouldn't learn his fate until Carpenter pressed Play.

Sam comes over to update me on some things he has been working on.

He doesn't predict that I'm going to like what he's going to say, which he always does when he has something good for me. But he doesn't warn me that I'm going to hate it, so I'm expecting something of no consequence.

That's exactly what I get.

"I've looked into Rayburn's finances as much as I can," he says. "I told you that in the past he's been strapped for cash, and that never really changed. If he was being paid a lot of money, it doesn't show up anywhere."

"That's unfortunate."

"And the same thing is true for Mullens. But keep in mind, these were highly sophisticated computer guys. They would have been capable of hiding money; maybe it's in crypto, which is a whole different ball game."

"Sharon Keller said you could buy things in the metaverse using crypto," I say.

Sam nods. "There you go. Rayburn could have been the Warren Buffett of the metaverse and I wouldn't know it."

"Okay. What else have you got?"

"There was a phone call from campus to BJ's phone on the day of the murder, so it could have been the clerk telling him that Rayburn wanted him to come to his house."

"Was it from the clerk's phone?"

"Impossible to tell; it was through the university switchboard. It literally could have come from any landline on campus."

"Damn. You got anything good to report?"

"Decent. The two creeps from the metaverse who we nailed are in jail without bail. Turns out they have a bunch of priors; they could be going away for a long time."

"I'll call Sharon and tell her. She'll be happy to hear it. Those guys messed with the wrong avatar."

Sam nods. "That's for sure. I got their computer; Rayburn really screwed it up good. I can't even tell what he did. There's no virus in there, but it's shut down."

"They also messed with the wrong professor."

"I've done some research on where the metaverse is going. There are predictions that by 2030 people will be spending three hours a day in there. For kids it will be the equivalent of ultimately spending ten years of their life in virtual reality."

"Life as a video game," I say. "I'm planning to stay in real reality . . . unless the NFL moves over there."

"You think the Giants would do any better virtually?"

"Only if they pick a quarterback in the avatar draft."

When Sam leaves, I call Sharon Keller at her home in Colorado. She is obviously surprised to hear from me. "Mr. Carpenter . . . Andy . . . is everything okay?"

I must be associated with bad news. "Everything is fine. I just wanted you to know that those two guys that bothered you are in jail. They were denied bail and are very unlikely to do well at trial."

"You think so? I can't help it; I still worry about what they might do."

"You can stop worrying. Committing the crime on videotape is not the best approach to take if you want to stay out of prison."

"That's a relief. I mean, they don't know my real name or where I live, I know that, but it still makes me nervous."

"Have you gone back into the metaverse again?" I ask, hoping she'll say no.

"I have. I know that isn't smart, but at first I wanted to see if those two guys were there. They weren't, so I stayed for a while, and I got hooked again. It's very easy to get hooked."

"That's what they're counting on." I don't even know who I mean by *they*; I guess I imagine a council of evil metaversians trying to lure people into their world.

"I did see the third person, the one Steven couldn't identify," Sharon says. "But he was behaved and didn't bother me."

"You might want to steer clear of him."

"I will do my best, but it's hard. He spoke to me a couple of times . . . asked me if I was going to the quad. But I just said no and walked away."

"What's the quad?"

"There's a general large area where people meet. I hadn't known what people called it before."

"Okay, just be careful. And I'll update you when I hear more about the other two guys."

"Thank you. Thank you for everything, Andy."

"This is Gregori Borodin" are the words that the voice on the other end says after I say, "Hello."

A phone call from Borodin is not something I was prepared for; I just got back from my morning walk with the dogs and was planning my day. I've got a feeling this call is going to change my plans.

"Well . . . Borodin." I've had better comebacks in my day.

"We need to meet."

So far he's dominated the conversation while using just eight words. "For what purpose?"

"You'll find out when we meet. You pick the place and time."

In times like these, my dominant instinct is for self-preservation. That instinct is telling me not to take this meeting at all, but I realize I have to. So I want to pick the safest possible place and time, while insuring privacy.

"The tennis courts at Eastside Park in Paterson. Noon."

"Today?" he asks, surprised. "That's in ninety minutes."

"I'm aware of that."

"Tennis courts at Eastside Park . . . in ninety minutes. Be prepared, I will need to confirm that you are not using a recording device."

"That's fine. I won't be."

Click.

There were three reasons I set the meeting for so soon. One is that it gives him less time to set up some kind of violent encounter, an ambush, as we used to say back in Dodge City. The second is that Laurie is in the next room and Marcus is in the den, since his job these days is to stay close and protect me. I believe Corey will be reachable as well, but even if not, I should be well-covered.

The third reason is now I only have ninety minutes to dread and be afraid, rather than a day or two if the meeting was delayed. That is not a small consideration.

The truth is that I doubt Borodin is planning to kill me, at least not now. He wouldn't have called and given me this heads-up; he would have tried to shoot me when I was out and about.

My guess, and that's all it is, is that he is going to threaten me, to warn me to back off. There is no chance of that.

Laurie calls Corey and explains the situation. Rather than come to the house, he is going to head straight to the park and make sure Borodin doesn't have people there to welcome me in an unpleasant fashion.

He will call and report in, whether or not he finds anything significant. We'll have plenty of time to abort should there be any danger awaiting me.

So the plan, such as it is, comes together quickly. First of all it has to, because the meeting time is so soon. But it's also because we have so little that we want to accomplish; all we want to do is listen to what he has to say without me getting killed, with an emphasis on me not getting killed.

Corey says there has been no activity near the tennis courts at all. That's no surprise, since it's eighteen degrees out and everything is covered with a few inches of snow. I wouldn't expect Novak Djokovic and Rafael Nadal to show up and play a five-setter.

I sit on the bench outside the courts. Marcus is about a dozen feet away from me; we've determined that he has to be close in case Borodin makes some kind of sudden move. Corey and Laurie have taken up positions much farther away; they're only noticeable because no other people are present. But from their vantage point they can see if anyone else shows up.

A car pulls up, and the driver, who seems to be alone, gets out. This must be Borodin. He is thirty yards away but looks huge and gets larger as he approaches. He looks like an Abrams tank with a narrow waistline.

He glances at Marcus as he passes him and comes up to me. "You're Carpenter," he says, his Russian accent obvious.

"What gave it away?"

"Stand up, I need to make sure you are not wired."

I do so, and he frisks me. I'm wearing a coat so I'm not sure how positive he can be in the results, but he seems satisfied. Then he indicates Marcus. "He needs to move away."

I shake my head. "No, he stays there."

"What I have to say is for your ears only. I can move him if I have to."

"You'd be surprised." Then, "Marcus, please take a couple of steps back."

Marcus does so, and I say, "Talk softly. He won't be able to hear you."

"Is he the one who neutralized my two men?" Borodin's referring to the two security guys with the drug dealer.

"He is. He's an outstanding neutralizer."

Borodin turns to Marcus. "We will meet when this is over, my friend."

Marcus doesn't respond. Marcus is much better at neutralizing than he is at responding.

"You want to get to the point?" I ask. "It's cold out here."

"You chose the location. I have a proposition for you. There is the distinct possibility that a man will soon confess to the murder of Steven Rayburn. He will be believable; the man has a violent background and no alibi. His confession will be impossible to disprove."

"Did he commit the murder?"

"That doesn't concern you."

"Let me take a wild guess. You want something from me in return for convincing this man to confess."

"Yes. Since your client will go free, you will have no further need to investigate myself or my associate. You will thus cease your efforts."

"And if I refuse your offer?"

"You will be making a serious mistake. Of that you can be certain."

"That sounds very much like a threat."

"We have no need to be adversaries. We agree on this arrangement and then we go our separate ways."

"Where is Mullens?"

Borodin smiles. "I don't know. He doesn't keep me informed as to his whereabouts."

"I want to talk to him."

"People don't always get what we want, except for me. I always get what I want. Now, are we agreed on our arrangement?"

"I'll need some time to think about it," I say, because I will.

"Shall we say eight tonight? That should provide ample thinking time."

I nod. "That's reasonable. How should I contact you?"

He thinks for a few moments. "If you agree to the proposition, then shortly before eight o'clock turn off the Christmas lights on the outside of your house. I assume you are aware Christmas has passed anyway?"

I don't think I'll discuss Laurie's Christmas issues with him. What concerns me more is he obviously has been to my house. "That works. If I agree, the lights will be off."

"And if the lights are off, we will move forward with our arrangement." He turns and walks past Marcus, staring at him the entire way. Then he goes to his car and drives off.

Everybody goes back to the house so I can download my conversation with Borodin to them.

It was not that long, so I am able to pretty much relate it verbatim. I even include the Marcus references, in case Marcus didn't hear it all. I want him to know that Borodin has vowed to meet up with him at some future time.

Marcus does not seem to panic at the news.

I should have asked Eddie Dowd to come over and give his opinion on this, since it is definitely a question of legal ethics. Legal ethics, as anyone who has seen me in a courtroom can attest, is not my strong point. I can fill Eddie in later if I can't come to a decision on my own.

But make no mistake; this is not an easy decision.

"What was your initial reaction?" Laurie asks. Her style is to come to conclusions in a rational and orderly fashion. I'm usually more shoot from the hip.

"My initial reaction was to tell him to shove it, but that's partially because of the source. The guy is as unlikable as anyone could be. Add to that the fact that he is almost definitely a murderer, and my instinct is to say no to anything he proposes, simply because he is the one proposing it."

"But?" she prompts.

"But my first obligation is to my client. If an opportunity presents itself that would exonerate him, how do I turn that down? I would not have to lie to the court; I wouldn't have to do anything. This other guy would confess, and I'd just have to show up at the jail with a suit of clothes so BJ could go home well-dressed."

"It's not that simple," Corey says. "Now I'm not a lawyer—"

I interrupt, "I'm envious of that."

He ignores me and continues, "But don't you have an ethical obligation to ensure that a fraud is not perpetrated on the court?"

"I don't know that it's a fraud. Maybe the guy who will confess actually did it. He obviously is connected to Borodin, and I doubt they were in the same Cub Scout troop."

"You know better than that," Laurie says.

I nod. "Then why would he confess?"

"Who knows?" Corey asks. "Maybe Borodin is going to take care of his family if he goes along. Or maybe he's threatened to kill his family if he doesn't. Either thing could get him to take the hit here."

"Frank Pentangeli went a step further," I say.

"Who is that?"

"A character in *The Godfather.* Tom Hagen talked him into slitting his wrists in a warm bath in return for Michael taking care of his family."

Laurie frowns. "You and *The Godfather* again."

"*The Godfather* is the most insightful piece of literature ever written. Throw in *Seinfeld* and you have the answer to every issue and problem society faces."

"Except this one," she says. "So let's get back to it."

"Okay. So I buy the ethical obligation argument to an extent; I think the confession will be a fraud."

"You also have a moral obligation not to let a murderer go free, which is what will happen if you let Borodin and Nucci off the hook," Laurie says.

"That I disagree with. It's not my job to put murderers in jail," I say. "It's my job to get nonmurderers out of jail."

"You can't be sure that's what will happen here," Corey says. "If the guy who confesses didn't actually do it, and we all agree that he probably didn't, then the cops could well see through it. And then you're back in a trial while having delayed the investigation maybe so long that it can't be revived successfully."

I nod. "True. So where are we?"

"You tell us," Laurie says.

"Okay, I think my ethical, and maybe moral, obligation is to turn down the deal. And, as Corey says, it might not achieve the desired outcome, which is to get BJ off the hook. However—and there is a however the size of Brazil—"

Laurie nods; she knows what's coming.

"—how am I going to feel if BJ gets convicted and goes off to spend most of the rest of his life in prison, when I might have been able to get him off? And that would also mean the real murderer would have gone free. How am I going to feel then?"

"Like shit," Laurie says.

I nod. "Sebastian never took a dump that big."

We leave the outside Christmas lights on as eight o'clock approaches.

I wish Borodin had suggested that we shut off the inside Christmas music as a signal; that I could have gone along with.

I watch out the window as he drives past the house and sees that the lights are still on. I assume he knew this was possible and has an alternative plan; I just wish I knew what it was.

I'm feeling a little sick to my stomach. I considered bringing BJ in on the decision, but opted against it. The obligations are mine, not his. I just hope he doesn't suffer for it. I am feeling unrelenting pressure to win this case, but it's not a question of the amount of effort that I and the team put in.

The effort will be there, but this case will rise or fall based on facts. Actually, facts won't be enough. I'll also have to make the jury believe them.

One area in which no progress is being made is the disappearance of Professor Samuel Mullens. We are getting discovery on that police investigation; we requested it because Mullens was on our witness list and is integral to our case.

The police are nowhere; they can't even decide if Mullens left voluntarily or was kidnapped. My suspicion is the latter; I can't see Mullens throwing away his career on such an erratic move. But that he left having packed his things and taken his computer is definitely causing the investigation to move forward at less than full-tilt.

The question for me is not whether Mullens was kidnapped; it is whether he is still among the living. I'm betting he is, especially after Borodin's offer to me. They are worried that whatever they are doing could be disrupted. And if it is still ongoing and not yet accomplished, then I assume they still need Mullens.

But the cops apparently have no clue as to where he could be, which doesn't surprise me. With Nucci and Borodin's resources, Mullens could be in Moscow sucking down borscht and playing video games.

We need to get the cops more focused on finding him, and Corey and Laurie have been making calls to their former colleagues in the department. But so far it has not achieved any results.

If Mullens is alive, he's most likely in a bad spot. He's got to give them what they want, but if he does, he will no longer be useful to them. If he has any doubts about what that will mean, he only has to think back on his pal Steven Rayburn.

As for myself, I still don't think I am in any personal danger. For Nucci and Borodin, this entire thing has been about minimizing the attention paid to Rayburn's murder. That was the purpose in hiring Howarth and getting him to represent BJ.

To kill me, with the trial imminent, would be to shine an intense media spotlight on it, which would be counterproductive for them. It wouldn't be so great for me either.

Of course Laurie feels differently, and I know she is having Marcus watch over me. I can't stop her, or him, and I probably shouldn't want to.

My best guess is that they will lie low, let the trial come and go, and then the pressure will be off them. That will especially be true if BJ gets convicted, but to some degree it will be true either way.

I'm not ready for trial, but then again I never believe that I am.

Unfortunately, judges never consult with me to ask if I'm ready or to solicitously give me more time.

They bang their gavel and start the process.

I've got a story for you, but you have to do something for me," I say to Vince Sanders.

I've called him to my office with the story promise, but he senses that he's not going to like the quid pro quo.

"First tell me, is the free food and beer in jeopardy?" he asks. "Because if it is, I think Pete should be involved."

"No, I'm not that kind of guy."

"Since when?"

"I've always been a good guy, despite what Pete says. But I want to give you an exclusive as to the defense strategy in the Rayburn murder case."

"Why?" Vince is suspicious but I can tell he's also eager. The case has become a pretty big deal throughout the metropolitan area.

"Because the last time you broke a big story Hula-Hoops were a thing, and I am trying to resurrect your career."

"I repeat, why? More important . . . what do I have to do in return?"

"The defense strategy is to tie Thomas Nucci to the murder, so when you run it, you have to use a good part of the story that your reporter Mariah Covey wrote about him. The piece her previous editor wouldn't publish."

"Again, why?"

"This part is off-the-record. I want the jury to know who Nucci is, in case I have trouble getting his reputation admitted through witness testimony. Then I'll bring it up during the trial. Your story will get a second life; it will actually become part of the story."

Vince thinks about it for a few moments and smiles. "I think I can live with this."

Vince's story ran yesterday as it was supposed to. He let me pick the date, and I chose the day before today's jury selection.

There is no way to know how many people read it; it's not like there are Nielsen numbers reported the next morning. But as I hoped, it did prompt other media outlets to comment on it, which increases the effective reach well beyond that of Vince's newspaper.

My goal, of course, was to make sure the prospective jurors either saw it or were aware of it. So when the first juror took the stand for voir dire, I asked, "Have you heard of Thomas Nucci?"

"Yes," he said.

"Have you read a story about him recently in the newspaper or heard about that story through other media?"

Nabers immediately objected and Judge Lockett sent the jurors out of the courtroom so we could argue it out. I was glad he didn't call for the discussion to be in chambers or in a sidebar because I wanted the media in the gallery to hear it and report on it.

"Your Honor, Mr. Nucci is not a part of this trial," Nabers said.

I smiled. "He will be."

"This is a clear attempt by the defense, as was yesterday's article, to implicate Mr. Nucci in this murder despite all the evidence pointing to the defendant. I think Mr. Carpenter should be sanctioned for planting this in the media."

The judge turned to me. "Mr. Carpenter? I assume you have a different point of view?"

"Very much so, on all counts. First of all, Your Honor has never issued a gag order nor admonished counsel not to talk to the press. In fact, Mr. Nabers called a press conference when Mr. Bremer was arrested. I don't recall him asking you to impose sanctions at that time.

"Secondly, it is the first time in my career that a prosecutor has objected to my previewing the defense case in advance. Most of them would welcome it as a guide on how to counter it.

"Thirdly, I have not chosen Mr. Nucci's name out of thin air. The defense will be presenting evidence directly linking him to this crime. This is clearly allowed when the defense is demonstrating third-party culpability.

"I would have thought that Mr. Nabers knew that principle of the law. Had I known otherwise I would have spelled it out earlier."

"Your Honor, that is an outrageous ad hominem attack," Nabers said.

"Confine your arguments to the facts, Mr. Carpenter. No personal references in my courtroom."

"I apologize to the court and counsel," I say, even though

I am not in the slightest bit sorry. I want to get under Nabers's skin, which is not proving particularly difficult.

"I'll allow the voir dire questioning," the judge says. "Objection overruled."

He brought the jurors back in and I asked the same question of every one to follow. Many of them had not seen or heard about the article, but I'm betting they're going to go home and google it.

Selection ended with the mandatory twelve people and three alternates. I hope we did well, but I can't be sure. I can never be sure. Prospective jurors come in with an agenda: some want to be chosen and some don't. Often they tailor their answers in voir dire to what they think will further those goals.

BJ periodically asked me how we were doing, and each time I said that I had no idea, that we'd know when they delivered a verdict. Tired of my nonanswer, he started asking Eddie, but didn't get much insight there either.

Bottom line is that anyone who doesn't think jury selection is a crapshoot has never played craps.

The timing of the day is not working out for us. There is enough time left for Nabers to deliver his opening statement, but possibly not enough for me to follow with mine. I hate leaving the jury spending the night having heard only one side to the story, and I ask Judge Lockett to push everything back to the morning. He turns me down.

"Ladies and gentlemen, I want to start by thanking you for being here, for performing this service for your community," Nabers starts. "It is not easy; it takes time and effort and concentration and a willingness to sacrifice, and yet you have all signed up for it. I appreciate it, and though I can't speak for him, I suspect Mr. Carpenter feels the same way.

"This case is not a complicated one; in fact it is not an unusual one. Two people had an argument and one of them decided to exact vengeance. He killed the other person, in this case by smashing him over the head with a metal statue. He did it from behind; the victim would literally have not known what hit him.

"Things like this happen all too frequently; sometimes it takes the form of road rage. An argument that should be over and done with causes someone unstable to react violently.

"We will show that Brian Bremer and Professor Steven Rayburn had such an argument. It should not have been a very big deal, but Bremer could not get it out of his mind. So two nights later he went to Professor Rayburn's house and exacted his revenge.

"After doing what he did, he calmly ransacked the house and smashed Professor Rayburn's computer. There is no way to know if he planned to do that originally, or if those actions were a cover to make it look as if an intruder committed a robbery gone bad.

"But either way, he couldn't resist actually taking something . . . a valuable watch and six hundred dollars in cash. He put those things in his car and then went back inside; he claimed later he was going to call nine-one-one and report finding Professor Rayburn dead when he arrived.

"He never got to make the call, if that was his intent. The police had been alerted by a neighbor who heard an argument, and they arrived and found Mr. Bremer next to the body, with the victim's blood on him. The stolen merchandise was recovered and Mr. Bremer arrested.

"You should not take my word for any of this. What I just said was not evidence, it was just words coming from an advocate's mouth. You need not give it any weight. But when I prove what I said with actual evidence, then you should give that a hell of a lot of weight.

"I should warn you that during this trial you are going to see some unpleasant photographs. There is simply no way around that. Murder is never pretty and this one was particularly brutal.

"I should also warn you that the defense will be presenting some far-out conspiracy theories in an effort to distract you from the obvious truth. All I ask is that you keep your eye on the ball, and on the facts.

"Thank you again for your invaluable service."

Once Nabers sits down, Judge Lockett turns to me and says that the day is getting late. He asks if there is enough time for me to give my opening, or would I prefer to wait until the morning.

"I'd prefer now, Your Honor. I will be relatively brief."

He nods, and I begin, "Ladies and gentlemen, thank you for being here and thank you for doing this. I agree with Mr. Nabers that this is an imposition that we must ask of our citizens for the justice system to function. What you are doing is indispensable.

"Have you ever seen a play, or movie, or read a book,

in which everything seems totally real, but you know it's fiction? You know it's just a story that someone made up?

"That's what just happened in this courtroom. Mr. Nabers told you a story. I have no doubt that he believes it; but it is fiction. And like the book or movie or play, it has been written in such a way as to get you, and the police, and Mr. Nabers, to believe it. But that doesn't make it true.

"Mr. Bremer is an outstanding student and fine young man who has never been in any kind of trouble, ever. You won't hear Mr. Nabers point to a past offense on Mr. Bremer's record, because there is none.

"He had a minor argument with a professor over a grade on a quiz, so he smashed his skull with a statue? It is preposterous on its face.

"Mr. Nabers told you that this case is not complicated. That is not true; it is very much so. He wants you to take the story at face value; the way it appears on the surface. But I will show you what is underneath, I will show you the forces that took great pains to frame Mr. Bremer, and I will show you why they did it.

"The prosecution will not go there. The police put on blinders from the first minute of the case and never took them off. They found the clues they were supposed to find, then nodded and said, 'Let's move on. Next case.'

"You are here because they believed the story that they were told, the story they are presenting to you. We will show why they were wrong to do so, and why the wrong man is spending his days in jail, waiting to be exonerated.

"Thank you for listening."

I head back to the defense table. BJ's expression is

impassive, as I have told him to remain throughout the trial. Doris Bremer is in the front row, and she nods her approval to me.

She is counting on me to give her back her son. That pretty much defines the word *pressure.*

Nabers calls Sergeant Alan Vaccaro as his first witness. Vaccaro is but the first example of a disadvantage I will face; I don't know him at all.

Middlesex County is just not a place where I am familiar with the people at any level of the justice system. Back in my home base of Passaic County the opposite is true, and I am able to take advantage of personal vulnerabilities that I am aware of. That's not going to happen here.

Sergeant Vaccaro was one of the first cops on the scene at Steven Rayburn's house the night of the murder. There were others with him, but Vaccaro is a veteran of ten years on the force, and I suspect that Nabers considers him the best spokesman for the group. I'm sure he must have countless hours of testifying under his belt.

Once Nabers has let Vaccaro describe his experience and commendations, Nabers asks him if he arrived at the Rayburn house that night.

"Yes, sir. Myself and three other officers were the first to arrive."

"Why did you go there?"

"A nine-one-one call was made by a neighbor indicating that he heard a potentially violent argument taking place."

"How long after receiving the call did you arrive?"

"About four minutes."

"Did you ring the bell? Knock on the door?"

"Yes, both, but no one answered," Vaccaro says. "Believing that a crime could be in progress or someone could be in danger, we went in."

"What did you find?"

"Professor Rayburn was on the floor, bleeding from an obvious head wound. The defendant, Brian Bremer, was standing about three feet from the body. He was holding a cell phone."

"What did you do?"

"I told him to drop to the floor. I needed to assess the situation, and to confirm that he was not armed. I then felt for a pulse on Professor Rayburn but did not detect any.

"The wound certainly appeared likely to be fatal. Another officer immediately called for an ambulance and for homicide detectives to come to the scene."

"Did Mr. Bremer obey your command to go to the floor?" Nabers asks.

"He did."

"Was he armed?"

"No, sir. We searched him for weapons; frisked him and had him empty his pockets."

"Did you see anything that you considered might be the murder weapon?"

"Yes. There was a metal statue on the floor near the body."

Nabers uses this opportunity to show a photo of the body with the statue nearby. There is a significant amount of blood and the head injury looks horrible, which is why Nabers will make sure the jury sees it many times.

It is designed to sicken and outrage them and to make them want to put away the person who did it. Since BJ is the only one charged, they will undoubtedly look to him.

"Did you place Mr. Bremer under arrest?" Nabers asks.

"We did not. We waited for homicide detectives to arrive, and they questioned him."

Nabers turns the witness over to me. He did not do us much damage, and I think I can make some headway in my cross-examination.

"Sergeant, you said that a neighbor called nine-one-one, but you neglected to mention the neighbor's name. Can you do so now?"

"No, it was phoned in anonymously. That frequently happens; people don't want to be involved."

"When I call someone, caller ID tells them that it's me calling. In this case, with all the resources of the police department, the call could be traced, could it not?"

"Perhaps, I don't know. I do not know the man's name."

"Do you even know if it was a neighbor?"

"That's what he said."

"Could he have been calling from in front of the house?" I ask.

"It's certainly possible."

"Or down the street?"

"Possible."

"Or Connecticut? Or North Dakota? Or Argentina?"

"I really couldn't say where he was calling from," Vaccaro

says. "But he had to be close enough to have heard the argument."

"Unless he lied about hearing an argument at all," I say, not really asking a question, but hoping for an answer.

"He said he heard an argument."

"Right. And you know this person doesn't lie, you just have no idea who he is."

"The result is consistent with there having been an argument," Vaccaro says.

"We'll get a chance to find out. So just to confirm, Mr. Bremer was not armed, had a phone in his hand, and was cooperative?"

"Yes."

"And when you frisked him for weapons and had him empty his pockets, did you find any stolen merchandise?"

"No."

"Mr. Nabers mentioned a watch and cash in his opening statement. Mr. Bremer did not have that in his possession when you searched him?"

"No."

"So he didn't steal anything?"

"I wouldn't say that. He could easily have put merchandise in his car and come back in the house."

There is much more I could try to get out of Vaccaro, but I want to hold my ammunition until I can use it on future witnesses who could do us more damage.

"I see. No further questions."

Though they were telling him otherwise, Samuel Mullens knew that effectively he had been kidnapped.

He was never alone; the house he was in had at least three other men in it at all times. They were all Russian and they were all obviously dangerous.

He had not been allowed to leave; food was brought to him and was plentiful. But they were always watching him; there was no chance he could make a break for it.

They were his captors.

One of the men with him was obviously computer proficient, though undoubtedly not in Mullens's class, and certainly not possessing anywhere near the capability of the late Steven Rayburn.

Mullens's computer had been gone over by the man, and the email and message apps were removed, preventing Mullens from communicating with the outside world. The screen mirroring function had been turned on, so the man could make sure that Mullens was not trying to circumvent that isolation. Mullens's phone had also been taken from him and turned off, so it could not emit a GPS signal.

Borodin had been to the house a number of times, to

ask him about his progress. Nucci had not been there at all, or at least Mullens hadn't seen him.

The hardest part for Mullens was maintaining the charade that he was trying to solve the computer problem. Rayburn had already solved it, but the captors did not know that, and he could not tell them. He had no doubt he would be killed, as had happened to Rayburn.

As Mullens saw it, as long as they thought they needed him, he was safe.

So the days went by and Mullens had to appear to be working toward the computer solution. There had to be a limit to Borodin's patience, but Mullens could not predict when that limit would be reached. But Borodin's patience would not be infinite.

Mullens knew that somehow he had to get away before that point.

His life depended on it.

Next up for Nabers is Sergeant Marcia Kendrick, another longtime veteran, this time in forensics.

Sergeant Kendrick and her team were part of the army of police personnel who'd descended on the Rayburn house once the body was discovered, a fact that Nabers quickly has her point out to the jury.

Of course, he shows two more photographs of the scene before questioning her about it.

"Obviously there was a great deal of blood," Nabers says.

Even though that wasn't actually a question, she says, "Yes."

"Whose blood was it?"

"Professor Rayburn's."

"Did tests show anyone else's blood?"

"No."

"Where was that blood?"

"On the victim's skin and clothing, on the floor, some spatters on the nearby walls, on the defendant's clothing and on his hands."

He moves on to fingerprint evidence and she says that she found BJ's fingerprints on the front doorknob and on a shelf not far from the body.

"Did you find any other prints?"

"Yes. They belonged to Professor Stephen Mullens, Adam Lusk, Sarah Rogers, Walter Thompson, and, of course, Professor Rayburn himself."

She identifies them for the jury: Mullens as another professor at Rutgers, Lusk as his assistant and TA, Rogers as his weekly housekeeper, and Thompson as a handyman supplied by the school to fix things around the house.

"Did you examine the metal statue found on the floor near the body?"

"Yes. It contained blood, hair, scalp and brain tissue, all from Professor Rayburn."

"Fingerprints?"

She shakes her head. "None."

"Was there a shelf it could have fallen from?"

"Not at a close enough distance."

"So whoever used the statue to commit the murder had wiped the prints off?"

"Or perhaps used gloves."

"Thank you. No further questions."

I start the cross with "Sergeant Kendrick, let's first talk about the fingerprints you found in the house. Did any of them surprise you? I mean, you would expect his assistant, his colleague, his housekeeper, and his handyman all to have left prints. Correct?"

"I would think so."

"And it's no surprise that Mr. Bremer's prints were there, since it's clear he was there when the police arrived, correct?"

"Correct. Not a surprise."

"You said you found Mr. Bremer's prints on the front doorknob. Was that on the inside or outside?"

"Outside."

"None on the inside?"

"No."

"Are you aware that in Sergeant Vaccaro's testimony, he said the police theory for why Mr. Bremer did not have the stolen watch and money in his possession was that he went outside and put them in his car?"

"I am not aware of what he testified to. I was not in the courtroom."

"Fair enough. If he testified to that, and if he is correct, how is it possible that Mr. Bremer's prints were not on the inside knob? Would he have gone out the window?"

"Perhaps he wiped the prints off."

I nod as if that clears everything up. "So he left the prints on the outside knob, but wiped the inside one. Maybe he thought that would be enough to fool the detectives, make them believe he wasn't there, even though he was there when they arrived, with his cell phone in his hand?"

"People who commit crimes make mistakes."

"As do people trying to solve them."

Nabers objects and Lockett sustains it and strikes my comment from the record.

"Let's talk about the blood that was on Mr. Bremer's clothes and hands. Are you aware that Sergeant Vaccaro ordered Mr. Bremer down to the blood-soaked floor?"

"Yes."

"That would explain him having blood on him, would it not?"

"Of course. But he obviously could have gotten it on him before he went to the floor as well."

"How tall was Professor Rayburn?"

"Six foot one," she says.

I show her a photograph that Nabers had shown her of the scene, which showed blood splatter on the wall from the blow to the head.

"The splatter was high up, correct? As it should have been with the victim getting hit on the top of his head."

"Yes."

"Did Mr. Bremer have blood on his face?"

"No."

"In his hair?"

"No."

"Yet if he had hit Professor Rayburn with that statue, he would have to have been very close to him. Isn't that right?"

"Yes."

"Thank you. No further questions."

Day one of the case went reasonably well.

I poked a few holes in the prosecution's case, but I am not having trouble containing my enthusiasm. That's because their case is puncture-proof.

No matter what I say, no matter how many semantic arguments I might win, the facts don't change. BJ was caught in Rayburn's house with the victim's blood on him, and then the stolen merchandise was found in his house.

It's all well and good for me to say someone else could have done it, but I'd better deliver the goods. The jury is going to want to blame someone for this vicious attack, and I am going to have to offer them a credible alternative.

I call Eddie Dowd and ask him to deliver a subpoena to James Howarth to compel him to show up to court to testify when called. He is my key link to Thomas Nucci and Gregori Borodin. They hired him to represent BJ and bury his case; it will not be hard to convince a jury that they did not do it out of the warmth of their hearts.

Howarth is in a difficult place. His choice is to make enemies out of Nucci and Borodin by testifying truthfully, or to make enemies out of Nucci and Borodin by perjuring himself and then having our phone conversation tape played.

I suppose a third choice would be to disappear until the trial is over, but then he would be violating a lawful subpoena, and I would make sure the tape is played anyway. If the judge for some reason deemed it inadmissible, I would make sure it is released to the public.

I don't feel remotely guilty about putting Howarth in this position. In return for cash, he was planning to set it up so that BJ went to prison for most of the rest of his life. If there is a more horrible thing a lawyer can do, I'm not sure what it might be.

A key for the defense is Professor Mullens. The cops seem no closer to finding him, and that could be because he is no longer alive. But if I'm right, Borodin and Nucci haven't killed him because they need him. That's why they let him take his computer . . . or at least I think so.

It is crucial that we find him, hopefully alive. But if he's dead, then even finding his body, harsh as it sounds, would be a plus for our side. If Rayburn's colleague is killed, then it obviously shows the jury that someone not named BJ is out there murdering professors.

I have an idea. . . . Actually, calling it an idea might be giving it too much credit. But I call Sam to run it by him.

"Sam, Mullens has his computer with him. If it's turned on and he's working on it, is there any way to track it and locate him?"

"What do you mean?"

"Sort of like the way you can find a phone."

"His phone has been turned off," Sam says.

"I know. But can a computer be traced the same way?"

"A phone has a GPS tracker in it; a computer does not."

"So there's no way to find it?"

"There's no way to find it."

"Thanks, Sam. That's what I thought. Wonderful chatting with you."

Walter Halitsky is the medical examiner for Middlesex County.

As medical examiners go, he is semi-famous. He's often a talking head on CNN and other news programs when a story requires his kind of expertise.

I have no idea why they choose him. He's not particularly charming. He's definitely not young and good-looking; Halitsky is in his sixties with a face that looks like he has spent the last thirty years scuba diving 24-7. He also has a raspy, off-putting voice, and a name that doesn't exactly roll off the tongue.

He must have a great publicity agent.

Halitsky performed the autopsy on Steven Rayburn. It wasn't his greatest challenge; the victim had a horribly smashed head, and Halitsky determined that he died of a horribly smashed head.

He has been the Middlesex County medical examiner for thirty-one years, and it feels like it takes that long for Nabers to demonstrate his credentials and experience to the jury. Nabers makes particular reference to Halitsky's television appearances, and some of the jurors nod in recognition. They've clearly seen him on TV, which gives him additional, unwarranted credibility.

Once they get into the specifics of the case, Nabers is fairly quick to get to the point. He asks Halitsky the cause of death, and the answer is "Blunt-force trauma to the rear and top of the skull."

"Would death have been instantaneous?"

"No question about it. The brain sustained catastrophic damage; function would have ceased virtually on impact."

"Did you examine the metal statue that was found on the floor?"

Halitsky nods. "Yes, I did."

"Is it your considered opinion that it was the murder weapon?"

Halitsky nods. "Certainly checks all the boxes. It had blood, fragments of the skull, and brain matter on it. It was solid enough to have done the damage as well."

"Do you have a point of view as to where the attacker was when he struck?"

"Yes. He was behind the victim."

"And great force was used?"

"Oh, yes. The attacker was either quite strong or very angry. Or both."

"Thank you."

Halitsky did us no damage, unless you count that Nabers got to show more gory photos to the jury. But I think the impact of that may be wearing off.

The truth is that the jurors learned nothing from Halitsky's testimony; before he took the stand they already knew that Rayburn died as a result of being smashed in the head by the metal statue. Halitsky didn't advance the ball in that regard and also said nothing to implicate BJ.

But I have something to gain from Halitsky, and Nabers knows it. He also knows that I would get it whether he called Halitsky or not. What surprises me is that he didn't bring it out himself, when it could have been couched in a way least damaging to the prosecution.

I hand Halitsky his autopsy report and I direct him to the third page, fourth paragraph. I have him read it; it contains some technical terms, so I ask him to put it in language that I and the jurors can more easily understand.

"There were methamphetamines found in the blood of the deceased."

"Illegal drugs?" I ask.

"Yes."

"A stimulant?"

"Yes."

"Could there have been a medical reason he was taking such a drug? Perhaps some ailment that he was treating?"

"No; the drug has no medicinal purpose."

"So is it fair to say this was not a drug that Professor Rayburn got by prescription?"

"That is fair to say."

"Based on the amount in his system, is it possible to tell when he last took that drug?" I ask.

"Not with any precision; I would have to know when he took it. But it was very likely within the previous twenty-four hours."

"Is it possible to say whether Professor Rayburn was addicted to this drug?"

"It is not possible to know that based on available evidence, but it is a very addictive drug."

"Thank you. No further questions."

Once again I've had some success, in this case by planting in the jurors' minds that by taking illegal drugs, Rayburn must have been buying them from some potentially dangerous entity.

It's a small positive, and one I'll expand on in the defense case. But it does not get us anywhere near the finish line. That line is looking farther and farther away as the time to present our case gets closer and closer.

During the lunch break I check my cell phone and there is a message from Sam that I may have given him an idea. He'll fill me in later.

That's good to hear, although I'm not sure what he could be talking about. I'm also not sure how I could be giving out ideas to other people when I am fresh out of them myself.

The afternoon session starts with Lieutenant Eugene Amos, the homicide detective who was in the lead on this case.

If central casting was asked to send down a tough, competent, no-nonsense cop, Amos is the guy they would send. Jurors will nod and agree with a guy like this because they'd be afraid not to.

Nabers spends little time on the murder scene; he asks Amos to describe the search warrant that was executed on BJ's home.

"We served it at eight o'clock in the morning. It entitled us to search the defendant's car and apartment."

"Was he home at the time?"

"Yes."

"What was his demeanor?"

"He seemed agitated."

I object, but Judge Lockett allows the question and answer to stay in the record.

"Did he offer any resistance?"

"No. He cooperated and left the premises, waiting with two of our officers outside in a patrol car as we conducted the search."

"What did you find that was of interest to you?"

"A Rolex watch and six hundred dollars in cash."

"Could that not have been the defendant's?"

"We considered that. It was hidden in a shoe in the closet, with clothes on top of it. But that could have been just to protect it from a possible burglary."

"What did you do?"

"First we asked the defendant if it was his and he said it was not. At that point we took him to the precinct for furthering questioning. A detective then took the watch to Professor Rayburn's assistant, a Mr. Lusk, who confirmed that he had a Rolex that looked like the one we had found.

"Subsequent investigation revealed that Professor Rayburn had owned the watch for more than a dozen years."

Unlike Nabers's direct examination of Amos, I am going to focus on the murder scene and not the execution of the search warrant. I know what they found there, I know Amos's description of it is accurate, and I'm not going to be able to challenge it, except for one thing that annoyed me.

"Lieutenant, you said that Mr. Bremer was agitated when you arrived at his house."

"That was my impression."

"Does it surprise you that a young man who is awakened by seven armed police officers at his house at that hour might seem agitated?"

"I would not say I was surprised, no."

"Thank you. Lieutenant, how long after the anonymous nine-one-one call did you arrive at the house?"

"Eighteen minutes. The patrol officers were on the scene far more quickly."

"Does it trouble you that the call was anonymous?"

"Not particularly. It turned out to be accurate in what it reported."

"Did you try to find out who made the call? Did you attempt to trace it? Did you canvass the neighborhood?"

"Yes, we tried unsuccessfully to trace it. We also went to all the houses that were in a distance from where loud arguing at the Rayburn house could be heard."

"And came up empty?"

He nods. "We came up empty."

"So is it your theory that the person who heard the arguing was out on the street, near the house? And that's how he heard it?"

"Yes, that's a working theory."

"Now we have heard testimony that it is also the police theory that Mr. Bremer committed the murder, put the stolen merchandise in his car, and then went back into the house."

"That's correct."

"Let's try some questions that call for yes-or-no answers, so please limit your answers to those two possible words. Okay?"

"Yes."

"Good. You obviously already have the hang of it. Did the anonymous caller, who conveniently must have been walking around with a cell phone that could not be traced, report seeing the defendant come outside?"

"No."

"So it doesn't trouble you that the caller was anonymous, that he had an untraceable cell phone, and that he didn't report the defendant coming out and returning?"

"No."

"Does it trouble you that no other neighbors heard any arguing?"

"No, it doesn't."

He used three words, but I let it go. "Does it trouble you that the defendant's prints were not on the inside door knob, as testified earlier, even though you believe he left the house and returned, closing that door from the inside?"

"No."

"Does it trouble you that the defendant had no blood on his face and hair, even though it has been demonstrated that the blood splatter was around that height?"

"No."

"Does it trouble you that the defendant has absolutely no history of violence or criminality of any kind?"

"No. There's a first time for everything."

"What does it take to trouble you, Lieutenant?"

Nabers objects, Judge Lockett sustains, and I withdraw the question. I let Amos off the stand, having made all my points.

Such as they are.

Since it's Friday and getting late, Judge Lockett announces that we are going to adjourn early for the weekend. That's fine with me; we'd be better off if he adjourned for a decade.

Before sending everyone home, the judge removes the

jury from the courtroom for the purpose of hearing a motion brought by Nabers. We had to disclose to him that James Howarth was given a subpoena to appear, and that is the subject of his motion.

Nabers knows why we are calling Howarth; I had to reveal it when I asked for BJ to be put in protective custody. By filing this motion, he is trying to prevent us from calling him.

He has no chance. He is trying to prohibit Howarth from testifying based on a violation of attorney-client privilege. I easily shoot that down by promising that not only will I not be disclosing communications between him and his then client, BJ, but that BJ has signed a waiver allowing it anyway.

Attorney-client privilege exists to protect the client, which is why the client has the power to waive it, as BJ has done.

Judge Lockett quickly recognizes that Nabers's position is untenable and rules against him. I'm actually pleased that he brought up the subject because the assembled press have witnessed it and will report on it.

I pat BJ on the shoulder and tell him to hang in there, and then Doris Bremer gives me a thumbs-up from her front-row seat.

Then we're off for the weekend. Nabers doesn't have many witnesses coming up; they will mostly be to motive and to Rayburn's good character.

And then it will be up to us.

There's another message from Sam on my phone when I get out of court: "I may be getting there . . . you're a genius. More later."

It's comforting to know that I'm a genius, and more comforting to know that Sam is making progress on something, but I have no idea what the hell he is talking about.

There's no sense calling and asking; Sam is not shy about sharing good news. He'll tell me the moment he has something, whatever that something might be.

For now all I can do is prepare to present our case. I've already made the key decision, which was a no-brainer. BJ himself is not going to testify; there is no upside to it.

All he can do is claim that he didn't do it, which the jury would properly see as self-serving. He has no information to provide that I can't get in through other witnesses; BJ does not have independent knowledge of what happened to Steven Rayburn. Worse yet, he would expose himself to potentially devastating cross-examination.

I've discussed it with him and he's agreed to waive his right to testify; he trusts me. I'm not so sure how trusting he would be if he knew that I turned down Borodin's deal, a deal that could possibly have freed him.

After dinner I head for the den to work on trial preparation. I have a Knicks game on as background noise; every time I look up, they are passing up sure layups to kick it out for a three-point miss. I don't understand modern basketball.

I head up to bed at around eleven. Laurie is already sleeping, but it takes me a while to get to sleep. I'm still feeling tremendous pressure as a result of turning down Borodin's offer. By now someone else could have confessed to the Rayburn murder, and there is a chance that BJ could be home feeding Murphy biscuits.

The phone rings; there is nothing louder or more jolting than a ringing phone in the middle of the night. I look at the clock and it says two thirty. It's still dark out, so I can't have slept until the afternoon.

"Hello?"

"Andy, it's Sam. I'm sorry to call so late, but I got something and I thought you'd want to know right away."

It better be good is what I'm thinking. "What is it?" is what I say.

"I may have found a way to locate Mullens. And it's all because of your idea. You want to hear it now? It's complicated."

"Sam, I'm not sure I can process 'complicated' right now. Can you be here in the morning? Maybe nine o'clock? Call Corey and Marcus and ask them to be here as well."

"Okay."

"But, Sam, wait until at least seven to call them, okay?"

"I will."

"Bye, Sam."

Laurie is awake and has heard my side of the conversation. "What did Sam want?"

"He may have found a way to find Mullens, which would be fantastic. I told him we'd talk about it in the morning."

"Smart move. Good night."

The dogs are walked, breakfast is eaten, and Laurie, Marcus, and Corey are here with me waiting to hear what Sam has to say.

It took me two hours to get back to sleep after he called last night, so if this is not really good, I mean extraordinarily good, I'm going to kill him. But when I get arrested, I'm going to find another lawyer to take my case.

"Thanks for coming, everyone. Sam has come up with something; he alerted me to that fact at two thirty in the morning. I should point out before turning the floor over to Sam that if what he has to say is not really good, I mean extraordinarily good, I'm going to kill him."

Sam smiles. "I am not worried. As you know, we, and I'm sure the police, have not been able to locate Samuel Mullens electronically. His phone has been turned off or destroyed, so there is no GPS to check. Borodin's phone has also been deactivated in some form, so if he has been with Mullens, we can't find him that way. These people are savvy when it comes to technology.

"So Andy asked me if I could find Mullens by locating his computer, which is generally impossible, since computers do not carry GPS devices.

"I have been emailing and messaging Mullens without any response, so that avenue was closed.

"Then I thought of LogMeIn."

Sam pronounces it as if it were three words . . . *log me in.* "I know what that is," I say, looking around for praise but getting ignored.

Sam nods. "Right. When you were on vacation before Christmas and you had the problem with your laptop, I took it over and fixed it from here."

"Yes," I say. "I sat there and watched you moving the cursor around on my screen. It was pretty cool."

"I was using LogMeIn. I figured that if Rayburn and Mullens were collaborating that closely, they must have been able to enter each other's computer in the same way. It would have made it much easier. And if they were doing it, there would be a record of it.

"So I cyber-entered the LogMeIn computer system and got Mullens's computer information."

Sam uses *cyber-entered* instead of *hacked.* He considers *hacked* an ugly word.

"But it was crucial that LogMeIn was still activated on Mullens's computer. I was hopeful that it would be, because there would be no reason to turn it off. It wouldn't affect what he is doing online.

"So I checked and it was in fact turned on, which allowed me to get his IP address. That tells me where he is, or at least where his computer is. That's the good news."

"What's the bad news?" Laurie asks.

"It's an inexact science and actually depends on the population density of the area that the address is in. For example, in New York City, it's very accurate. The more rural or lightly populated the area, the less precise it is."

"So where is he?" I ask.

"Pomona, New York. It's in Rockland County, about an hour from here. But I would say the computer is within a twelve-mile radius of the location I can provide. I can't pin it down more than that."

"Sam, this is great work. You can call me in the middle of the night anytime. Now how are we going to find this guy? And I don't have to tell you that we need to do it fast."

We all kick it around for a while and determine that Corey and Marcus will start by going up there to scout the area. Once we know the kind of situation we are dealing with, we will reconvene and come up with a plan.

Then, if we figure out where Mullens is, we will have to come up with another plan.

Then, if we get ahold of him, I will have to come up with a plan on how to get whatever we learn in front of the jury.

So many plans, so little time.

James Howarth is missing.

He didn't show up for a couple of court hearings on drug cases he was handling. When court personnel couldn't contact him, they went to his house. He appeared to have left quickly without taking much of anything.

The police are not considering it a missing person case yet; he's an adult and has not been gone long enough. But they will before long, especially since his car is still in his driveway.

I should have realized this would happen once we debated in open court Nabers's motion to prohibit Howarth's testimony. It made it into the media coverage and probably prompted Borodin and Nucci to take action.

I don't know for sure that it happened that way; it's possible that the subpoena panicked Howarth and he just took off. But I'm glad I'm not writing his life insurance policy.

Nucci and Borodin must not be aware that I have the taped phone conversation with Howarth. If they were, then they would realize that Howarth's presence in court is not necessary to show the jury that they were the people who hired him.

On a personal level, I realize that it was actions that

I took that put Howarth in whatever situation he is in. My entry into the case, then finding out Nucci and Borodin hired him, then trapping him with the taped phone call . . . it all led him to this point.

I don't take any great pleasure in it, but nor am I racked with guilt. Everything I did was in service of BJ's cause, which by any standard is a worthy one. And Howarth committed one of the worst sins a lawyer, or a human, could do: he was knowingly sending an innocent man to a lifetime in prison.

Unfortunately, I have to call Howarth early in the defense case. He provides the means by which I can introduce Nucci and Borodin; if not for their hiring of Howarth, I would have no way to make them relevant.

But at this point I'm not counting on Howarth's showing up; what I am counting on is convincing Judge Lockett to let me play the phone tape in Howarth's absence.

I'm hopeful the judge will allow it; I believe the law is in my favor.

What I am becoming less hopeful about is finding Samuel Mullens. Corey and Marcus spent a day scoping out the twelve-mile area in and around Pomona, and their report was not promising.

"I wouldn't describe it as rural," Corey said, "though some of it is. Mostly it consists of just neighborhoods, some upscale, some not. A lot of contemporary-style homes. There is a small retail area with a supermarket, a diner, and a few other stores, but the nearest large shopping area is in Spring Valley, which is outside the scope of our search."

"So no way to at least narrow it down?" I asked.

Corey frowned. "Very difficult. We can't go around randomly asking people questions. First of all, what are we going to ask them? If they've seen any bad guys hanging around? Secondly, asking questions would just attract attention and might scare off the people we're looking for."

"So how do we proceed?" Laurie asked.

"I hate to say it, but all we can do is spend time driving around looking for something, anything, that might tip us off. Maybe we'll see Borodin. We can certainly look for cars with Jersey plates, especially those that stay there for a long time.

"But there is always the danger that if we spend too much time driving around and canvassing the neighborhood, that in itself will attract unwanted attention, and some nervous resident might even call the police."

"I agree," I said. "Use Sam to alternate with you, and ask Willie Miller as well. He'd be very happy to help."

"Okay," Corey said.

"Let's hope we get lucky."

Unfortunately, that seems to be the defense strategy.

Nabers starts the week by calling Adam Lusk.

Nabers is doing it to establish motive, and doing it at this stage goes somewhat against the norm. Usually a prosecutor will show the motive before evidence about the crime. But in this case the motive is relatively weak, which may be why he chose to hold it back.

"What was your connection to Professor Rayburn?"

"I was assigned by the university to be his assistant. I also was a TA in his class."

"TA?"

"Teacher's assistant. I taught when he could not be there, helped grade papers, took student conferences, things like that."

"Are you a computer science student yourself?"

"Yes, on a graduate level. I have one more year to get my master's."

"Were you in the class the day that Professor Rayburn got into an argument with the defendant?"

"Yes."

"What happened?"

"Brian . . . the defendant . . . believed that he deserved a higher grade on a test than he received. He believed an answer was correct, but Professor Rayburn felt otherwise. I could describe the issue, but it was a very technical matter."

"I think we can all take your word for that," Nabers says, smiling. "So they argued about it in front of the class?"

"Yes. Brian was clearly upset, and that was increased by Professor Rayburn in my view being dismissive of him."

"So the grade was not changed?"

"It was not."

"Are you aware that Professor Rayburn, shortly after this incident, asked the department head to tell him the procedures for administrative discipline of a student?"

I object that Nabers is introducing facts not in evidence. It's a worthy objection, but Judge Lockett overrules it.

"I was not at the time, but I have since been made aware of it," Lusk says.

"Did you ever see Professor Rayburn using drugs?"

"I did not personally see him take any drugs, but there were times when it was obvious he was under the influence of something. And I certainly never smelled alcohol on his breath."

"Did it affect his work?"

"Never, at least not to my knowledge. He had a remarkable capacity to focus on his work; he let nothing interfere with that."

"Thank you. Your witness."

"Mr. Lusk, when this argument took place, did you move to break it up?" I ask.

"I did not."

"Did other students do so?"

"No."

"So there was no violence?"

Lusk shakes his head. "None."

"Slight pushing and shoving?"

"No."

"Personal attacks on each other's character?"

"No."

"Profanity?"

"None that I heard."

"So after it was over, neither you nor to your knowledge any students reported it to the school administration, or the campus police?"

"No."

"You weren't worried about it leading to violence?"

"It never entered my mind," Lusk says.

"You said you were aware that Professor Rayburn was asking questions about administrative discipline for students?"

"Yes."

"Did that have anything to do with Brian Bremer, if you know?"

"I have no idea."

"Do you know where Professor Rayburn procured his illegal drugs?"

"I do not."

"Thank you. No further questions."

I excuse Lusk, subject to recall in the defense case.

I call a sidebar and ask Judge Lockett for a continuance until tomorrow. "James Howarth was to be my first witness, and he was subject to a subpoena," I say. "As the court knows, he is missing and the police are now trying to find him. I would like to give them until tomorrow, and I need the time to restructure my witness order if they cannot."

Nabers objects, claiming that I have known Howarth was missing and should have prepared to go forward without him.

The judge grants the continuance, as I knew he would. It's only for one afternoon, and he recognizes the disadvantage to the defense to move forward. He also realizes that the issue of Howarth's being missing is not our fault.

The last thing the judge wants is to be overturned on appeal; so I was sure he would think there would be no downside to waiting until tomorrow.

I could use the time, but it's not to see if they are able to find Howarth.

I think he's dead.

I got no positive news last night from anyone.

Corey reported that he and the rest of the team have still gotten nowhere trying to locate Mullens in Pomona. Corey again says, no doubt correctly, that the only way they're going to find him is by getting a lucky break.

He also tells me that his contacts with the police have revealed that they are nowhere on the Mullens hunt as well. We haven't informed them about our belief that he is in Pomona; I'm afraid that their presence on the scene might cause the bad guys to get Mullens out of there or even kill him.

But if we can't get anywhere on that front, and soon, we may have to tell the cops about Pomona and hope for the best. Finding Mullens is that important.

Meanwhile, with Marcus off hunting for Mullens in Pomona, Laurie informs me that she has hired two ex-cops, guys she used to work for, to watch over me.

"That's crazy," I say. "Borodin would never try anything during the trial."

"I understand you're an expert on Borodin," she says, dripping sarcasm, "but just in case you happen to be wrong, you're protected. And so is this house, with Ricky in it."

She played the Ricky card, for which I have no defense, so I drop the argument. There was no chance I was going to win it anyway.

The police have also made no progress in finding James Howarth. I'm not sure how hard they are looking, since it's a defense attorney that is missing and a defense attorney that has been pushing them. But it doesn't matter; I know that the only way they're going to find Howarth is with a shovel.

I've decided regardless that Howarth has to be my first witness, or at least someone who might be considered a Howarth avatar. The star of the show will be the phone conversation.

I've prepared for this possible development, so I call retired state Supreme Court judge Nathan Arkin as my first witness. He is highly respected throughout the state, and I'm sure Judge Lockett must be very familiar with him, if not personally then by reputation. He defines credibility.

"Judge Arkin, did I ask you to listen to a tape recording of a phone conversation?"

"You did."

"Who was the conversation between?"

"Yourself and James Howarth, an attorney here in Middlesex County."

"What did James Howarth have to do with this case, if you know?"

"He was the attorney for the defendant, Brian Bremer, before you took over."

I introduce as defense exhibits two documents. One is from the phone company, confirming that a call took place at the time indicated between Howarth's phone and mine.

The other is a sworn statement from a voice-pattern expert that we hired confirming that the voice belongs to Howarth. He compared it to a Howarth voice sample from a conference he spoke at that we found on YouTube.

I tell the judge that I can introduce witnesses to support the authenticity of the documents. But because Judge Arkin says he has already talked to the relevant people, Judge Lockett is satisfied that it's not necessary, so I play the tape.

"Howarth."

"This is Andy Carpenter."

"What the hell do you want now?"

"I just wanted you to know that I'm going to subpoena you to testify at the trial."

"What?"

"You heard me. You're going to testify to the fact that Thomas Nucci and Gregori Borodin hired you to represent BJ, with instructions to get him to plead it out. And to make sure he loses at trial if he doesn't plead."

"This is bullshit. You swore you wouldn't tell anyone."

"No, I said I wouldn't tell Nucci. And I haven't. I'm a man of my word."

"There is no way I'm going to testify to this; Nucci would bury me if he finds out I told you."

"That's up to you, but you'll be under oath. Oh . . . there's one other thing I forgot to mention. I'm recording this call."

"You can't do this to me, Carpenter."

"Sure I can. New Jersey is a one-person consent state for taping calls, so it's completely legal. You're a lawyer; I would have thought you would know that."

The jury has listened intently to every word, as have the onlookers and press in the gallery. It is riveting stuff.

I turn to Judge Arkin, who has little to do and is being well paid to do it.

"As a respected former judge, is there any doubt in your mind that James Howarth just admitted that he was hired to represent Mr. Bremer by Thomas Nucci and Gregori Borodin?"

"No doubt at all."

"And did he also admit that he was hired with the instructions to either get Mr. Bremer to plead guilty or, failing that, to make sure he lost at trial?"

"Yes, he did."

"Did he voice fear that the fact he had admitted it would become known to Nucci and Borodin?"

"Yes, he did."

"Judge Arkin, if you know, was Mr. Howarth himself subpoenaed to testify at this trial, in front of this jury?"

"Yes, he was."

"Why is he not here then, pursuant to that subpoena?"

"I don't know that answer. According to the police captain I spoke with, he has disappeared under suspicious circumstances."

"Judge, do you have any familiarity with the Thomas Nucci that Mr. Howarth was talking about, was afraid of?"

Arkin nods. "Yes, he was to be a defendant in a murder case I was presiding over a few years ago."

"You say 'was to be a defendant'? Did the trial not take place?"

"It did not."

"Why not?"

"The main witness for the prosecution was murdered."

"Judge, did I ask you to look into companies that Thomas Nucci owns?"

"Yes, and I did so."

"Was one of them a software company that makes mostly gambling video games, and also antivirus applications?"

"Yes."

"Did you find the name Samuel Mullens connected in any way to that company?"

"Yes, he is listed on their website as a consultant."

"Who is Samuel Mullens?"

"He is a computer science professor at Rutgers University."

"So a colleague of Professor Rayburn?" I ask.

"Yes, and also a collaborator on research projects."

"Did I ask you to speak to Samuel Mullens about his connection to that company and his relationship with Thomas Nucci?"

"Yes, you did."

"And did you speak to him?"

"No. Mr. Mullens was reported missing last week and has not been heard from since. The police have been searching for him."

I pretend to look surprised. "So Mr. Howarth and Professor Mullens are both missing?"

"Yes."

"Thank you. No further questions."

There is simply very little for Nabers to get done on cross-examination. In terms of the phone tape, Judge Arkin was merely rubber-stamping something that the jury heard as clearly as he did. All the rest was just a recitation of facts.

But Nabers cannot let it all go unchallenged.

"Judge Arkin, do you have any knowledge as to whether Mr. Howarth has been the victim of foul play?"

"I do not."

"Do you know if his absence has anything to do with this trial?"

"I do not."

"Do you have any knowledge as to whether Professor Mullens has been the victim of foul play?"

"I do not."

"Do you know if his absence has anything to do with this trial?"

"I do not."

"Do you find it particularly surprising that a computer science professor would be a consultant to a software company?"

"I suppose not. It's an area I do not have a lot of expertise in. I have difficulty sending an email or texting."

Nabers smiles. "Join the club. Were there other academics listed on that website as consultants to the company?"

"Yes."

“How many businesses does Mr. Nucci own?”

“I found eleven.”

“Have any of those businesses been sanctioned in any way? Accused of fraud, perhaps?”

“Not to my knowledge.”

“Has Mr. Nucci ever been convicted of a crime, to your knowledge?”

“I don’t believe so.”

“Thank you, Judge.”

I have a quick lunch in the courthouse cafeteria with Lieutenant Luther Ellis of the New Jersey State Police.

I haven't had a chance to go over his testimony with him, though it's not going to be at all tricky. He's testified many times and knows the drill, and in this case he's just going to tell what he believes to be the truth.

"I'm not thrilled testifying for the defense," he says. "This is going to be hard to live down."

"I know, but in this case you're on the side of truth and justice."

"That's the side I'm always on."

"Right." There's no way I'm going to disagree with him just before I put him on the stand.

He looks down at his meat-loaf plate with disdain. "You eat this junk every day?"

"Since the trial started, I'm afraid so. Fortunately I don't usually try cases down here. Not that the Passaic County Courthouse has earned any stars from Michelin."

"I'll bet DoorDash would deliver stuff to you here."

"That's an idea," I say, because he really has given me an idea, but it's not the one he thinks. But it is one I need to get Sam working on fast.

"I use it every night," Ellis says. "The bad news is I've put on ten pounds."

We go over his testimony and then part ways. He'll stay out of the courtroom until summoned.

Meanwhile, I call Sam and say, "Sam, wherever Mullens is holed up, there must be other people with him."

"So?"

"So unless one of them is a chef, maybe they order in food?"

"It's possible. You mean like Grubhub or DoorDash or one of those things?"

"Or a local pizza place. Or a deli that delivers. Can you check it out?"

"Absolutely; almost all of these places are computerized now. I can check for patterns that fit what we are looking for. May take a little while, but I'll get back to you."

"We have very little time, Sam."

"I hear you."

When Lieutenant Ellis takes the stand, I ask him if he has ever heard of Professor Samuel Mullens.

"Yes. I'm leading the state police investigation into his disappearance, in coordination with local law enforcement."

"Any luck so far?"

"We have some leads we are following, but obviously none have borne fruit as of yet. I cannot comment on what those leads might be."

"I understand; it's an ongoing investigation." I still haven't told him that we have located Mullens's computer, and hopefully Mullens, somewhere in Pomona. I may have to, but I'm holding off as long as I can. "But have you discovered any connection between Professor Mullens and the late Professor Rayburn that you can share with us?"

"They were members of the same department at Rutgers. Beyond that, they were friends and collaborators on their scientific research."

"Professor Rayburn was a visiting professor from Georgetown, was he not?"

"He was, though shortly before his death he notified Rutgers that he would be leaving."

"Was that unexpected? Was the administration at Rutgers surprised by that?"

"Yes," Ellis says. "He was leaving prematurely."

"Almost as if he was afraid of something?"

Nabers objects, as he should. The question was out of bounds, which is why I asked it. I wanted the jury to hear it, and now they have. Judge Lockett sustains.

"We've heard testimony that Professor Mullens was a consultant to a company owned by Thomas Nucci. Were you aware of that?"

"Of course."

"Is Mr. Nucci part of your investigation?"

"Yes."

"Why?"

"Let's just say the department has had more than a passing interest in Mr. Nucci for a long time."

"Is that also true of Gregori Borodin?"

"Very much so, although that is more recent. Mr. Borodin became known to us about a year ago."

"Do you believe Professor Mullens is the victim of foul play? Perhaps kidnapped? Or worse?" I ask.

"I do."

"Can you explain why?"

"His disappearance is completely out of character; we have found no evidence he has ever done anything like this before. His friends and associates consider him to be very stable. Additionally, he has spent years earning tenure at Rutgers; to voluntarily put it at risk like this seems unlikely."

"Thank you, Lieutenant." I almost added, *Sorry about the meat loaf.*

Thomas Nucci and Gregori Borodin were both incredibly frustrated, but for very different reasons.

Nucci had never had an experience like he was going through. For years he had carefully cultivated an image of himself as a legitimate, successful businessman. Law enforcement knew better, but if he had any public image at all, it was one of respectability.

He had even come to believe it himself. His self-image was that of a CEO of many businesses, the head of a holding company that was a force to be reckoned with. That some of the organizations he oversaw were illegal did nothing to diminish his stature, at least not in his own eyes.

But now revelations from the Bremer trial were turning him into a mob boss in the eyes of the public. Every day now the media had him front and center; Carpenter was destroying what Nucci had spent years building. Yet there was nothing he could do about it.

And for what? The computer operation? It meant nothing to him beyond money. And while money was and remained a significant concern, it was not worth what he was going through.

Gregori Borodin's frustration came from an entirely different place. For him the operation was everything. It was a mandate from his bosses, and he had spent a huge amount of time and effort putting it together.

It had required a delicate touch, not something Borodin had ever been known for. He had had to do some coddling, a lot of deceiving, and of course some strong-arming and killing, but it had all come together.

Then Rayburn died and it started to unravel. Now they were depending on Mullens, and Borodin was growing increasingly concerned if Mullens could pull it off.

Borodin could read people extremely well, and he knew that Mullens was starting to panic. He believed it was causing Mullens to stall on the work because he was afraid that once he delivered, he would have outlived his usefulness.

He was certainly right about that.

Nucci was rapidly turning into another problem for Borodin to manage. In Borodin's view, Nucci was becoming unhinged and might do something dangerous. He had, for instance, floated the idea of killing Carpenter.

Borodin knew that would be a disaster and totally counterproductive. Not only would it ultimately not affect the trial, other than delaying it, but it would bring down overwhelming police and media scrutiny, something they could least afford.

He had gotten Nucci to back off on the idea of killing Carpenter, though truthfully promising Nucci that it would be first on Borodin's list when the operation was successfully concluded. But now Nucci was floating even wilder ideas, like killing Mullens and pulling the plug on the operation.

Nucci was no longer an asset. The reason that Borodin and the Russians had chosen him were no longer operative. They needed him to be a front, to hide their true reasons for wanting the operation to take place and succeed. He was also a link to Mullens, and therefore to Rayburn.

Rayburn, genius that he was, had been the key. Losing him was something that they never really recovered from.

Nucci had gone along because he wanted the money, and the muscle, and the Russians had both in great supply. He thought he could maintain his preeminent position, taking what the Russians had to offer while keeping them in their place.

He was wrong.

In Borodin's view, Nucci was the one who had made the key mistake—hiring Howarth. That trial was not going to pose a threat to them. The Bremer kid would have had an overworked public defender who would not have had nearly the resources to get anywhere near their operation.

But buying Howarth had brought in Carpenter and, even worse, had eventually shone a light on Howarth's connection to Nucci and Borodin. It was a disastrous move and Borodin should not have agreed to it. He blamed himself for doing so.

Add to that the constant pressure from Nucci to end the operation, and Borodin had had enough. Even more important, his bosses had had enough.

Borodin was a good soldier who always followed orders, and his bosses had ordered him to kill Thomas Nucci.

So that's what he did.

When I get up, Laurie is already riding on her exercise bike to nowhere.

She takes these spin classes through her video screen, which, as best I can tell, consist of a collection of lunatics, none of whom have an actual destination, but all of whom are into self-punishment.

They sing and encourage one another, waving towels in their glee as they pedal vigorously and unproductively. If aliens came down and watched a spin class, they would turn around and go home. These earthlings are nuts.

I let Sebastian lumber around in the backyard while I wake Ricky and then get dressed to take Tara and Hunter for our morning walk. By six thirty I'm out of the house with them.

Since I have to get to court, we take the short route and I'm back in about a half hour. As soon as I walk in, I hear Laurie calling me to come into the den. She's watching television and says, "Look at this," as she points to the screen.

The videotape playing shows a city street, I have no idea where, and includes cop cars with flashing lights. I wouldn't know why Laurie is interested in it if not for the chyron at the bottom that reads, "Thomas Nucci killed in hit-and-run accident."

I don't have to know anything more about it to be positive that *accident* is not the right word, and that Gregori Borodin is now totally in charge.

While showering and getting ready for court, I analyze the effect this will have on our case. It will not be terribly significant; I can just as easily paint Nucci as a villain now that he's dead as I could when he was alive.

The great villains of history are almost all dead, and nobody is giving them lifetime achievement awards.

If anything, it will help. The more violence that takes place while BJ is sitting in jail has to be a plus, unless you're a member of the Nucci family. If I can get the jury to hear about it, they will have to believe that a lot of dangerous people are involved in this case who are not sitting at the defense table, charged with murder.

I have some decisions to make. I have two other areas I can open up in demonstrating to the jury that there are other possibilities as to who might have killed Rayburn.

One is the drug dealer that Rayburn bought from. I am going to let the jury hear about him for a couple of reasons. One is that he is himself missing, having skipped bail. But the other is that I can tie Rayburn to him and the obvious danger inherent in that.

The other possibility, which I am still considering but may well reject, is having Sharon Keller talk about the guys who attacked her in the metaverse, and who subsequently threatened Laurie with a knife. We've flown her in and put her up in a hotel, and I told her to be ready in case I need her.

The two guys are in jail awaiting trial, and my being able to show that they had a grudge against Rayburn for destroying their devices makes them potential killers as well.

The truth is that I don't believe there is a chance in hell that either the drug dealer or the metaverse assholes killed Professor Steven Rayburn. My introducing them into this trial is simply to provide the jury with opportunities to have reasonable doubt, and to muddy the water with potential killers.

But even in addition to the fact that I'm sure none of those guys are the killer, a major negative is attached to this approach. I like to have one clear, coherent theory and stick to it; it's much cleaner and easier for the jury to understand. It also projects a confidence by the defense and avoids the chance that the jury will think we are throwing a bunch of things against the wall in the hope that something sticks.

Hovering over all of this is one disturbing fact. While I have shown a connection between Rayburn and Nucci, and while I have clearly shown Nucci and Borodin to be dangerous guys, I haven't yet offered an explanation for why they would have wanted Rayburn dead.

What could they possibly have gained from killing him?

And what were he and Rayburn working on that could have justified all this carnage?

I am no closer to answering those two questions than I was when Murphy showed up at our house.

My first witness for the day is a blood-splatter expert. I doubt that many kids grow up hoping to someday be a blood-splatter expert, but based on what he's charged me for this case, maybe they should. I think Ricky at this point wants to be an astronaut, but maybe I can get him to reconsider.

Basically he says that if Brian, or anyone, hit Rayburn in the head at the angle he was hit, he would have gotten blood on his face and in his hair. Even with me trying to move it along, his testimony, and the manner in which he speaks, are so dry I want to bring in a case of Evian for the jury.

Nabers makes some decent points in his cross-examination. Overall I think the witness's testimony is a positive for us, but it's certainly not going to carry the day.

During the break I reply to a message from Sam, who says he needs to talk to me right away. When I speak to him, he gets right to it.

"There's a food delivery service called Chow Down. It's based in New City, which is the town between Pomona and Spring Valley. They operate like DoorDash and the others, but it's local, not a chain."

"And? Sam, you need to get to the point quickly; I have to get back in court."

"And they've delivered three meals a day for the last two weeks to a house in Pomona."

"For how many people?"

"Four. Always four. And get this: they have instructions to wait outside and someone will come out to the street to get it. They're not to go to the door. The instructions say that there is someone ill inside, and they don't want the doorbell to disturb them."

"You got into their computer system?"

"Yes."

"Did you check who owns the house?"

"I did. It's registered in the name of Patrick Bernard. I looked into it and can't find a record of him anywhere. I think it's a fake name."

"This sounds like it, Sam. Please give the address to Corey and have him or Marcus check it out. Tell them to get some photos if it's possible without being noticed. Then let's all meet at my house tonight."

"Will do."

"Great work, Sam."

Sam's news means it's going to be hard for me to concentrate the rest of the court day, but I have to . . . that's why they pay me the big bucks. Or in this case, no bucks.

I call Sergeant Jeffrey Cook of Newark PD. Cook is the cop that Corey called to come and arrest the three drug guys after we raided their alley office.

I ask Cook to relate what happened the day and night of the raid.

"At about three P.M., I received a phone call from a friend, Corey Douglas."

"Who is Corey Douglas?"

"He's a former Paterson cop who is now an investigator for you."

"What did he want?"

"To inform me there was a good possibility that he would provide me with information about drug dealing that could result in an arrest. If it was going to happen, it would be that night, and I should stay ready."

"Did you?"

"Yes, I trust Corey completely. I recruited some officers and we waited for his call. It came at about ten thirty. He said I should go to a specific address and that there was no need to have weapons drawn, that the situation was well under control."

"So you went to that address?"

"Yes."

I show him photographs of the alley and office that make it look even seedier than it really was, and that is saying something.

Cook continues, "We found an office with you, Corey, and two partners of Corey's, Marcus Clark and Laurie Collins. We also found three suspects, two of whom were unconscious. The third, Rufus Aronde, appeared to be the leader of the group. We placed all three under arrest."

"Did you find and confiscate any merchandise?"

Cook nods. "Sixty-one thousand dollars in cash, and illegal drugs worth in excess of one hundred and fifty thousand dollars."

"Did it include methamphetamines?"

"It did."

I ask him to examine GPS records from Professor Rayburn's phone that we subpoenaed, which show that he was in that alleyway weekly. I also show Cook Uber records documenting his weekly trips to a location two blocks from the alley. They also coincide as far as date and time with the GPS phone records.

"Do you have any doubt that Professor Steven Rayburn was in that alleyway on a weekly basis?"

"No doubt at all."

"Can you think of any reason for him to be there other than to buy drugs?"

"I cannot."

"So Rufus Aronde and the two others were arrested. Are they in jail today?"

"Two of them are; Aronde is out on bail and has failed to report in as scheduled. Another warrant is out for his arrest, but he is currently missing."

"So James Howarth, Samuel Mullens, and Aronde are all mysteriously missing?"

Nabers objects that Cook has nothing to do with Mullens and Howarth, and Judge Lockett sustains. It's just as well, since as a Newark cop, Cook probably knows nothing at all about Howarth and Mullens.

"Sergeant Cook, in your investigation of this drug crime, are you looking into a possible relationship between Mr. Aronde and his organization and Thomas Nucci?"

"We are; we have information that Mr. Nucci controlled the entire operation."

"Where did you get that information?"

"An informant; I cannot reveal his name in open court."

"Understood. Are you planning to question Mr. Nucci?"

Nabers stands up to object, but before he can do so, Cook says, "Mr. Nucci was killed last night."

I can see Nabers wince slightly that the jury has now heard about Nucci's murder. There was nothing he could do to stop it; Cook got it in too quickly, just as I had hoped. I'm sure he will avoid mentioning it in his cross-examination; the last thing he'd want to do is call further attention to it.

Nabers gets right to the points he wants to make on his cross. "Sergeant Cook, do you have any information to make you believe that Mr. Aronde or his two associates killed Professor Samuel Rayburn?"

"No."

"Any information to make you believe they ordered the killing?"

"No. I don't know one way or the other. The Rayburn murder is not my case."

"To your knowledge, did Mr. Rayburn pay for the drugs?"

"I assume he did."

"And he was not in arrears? They weren't after him for nonpayment?"

"I have seen nothing to indicate that he was behind on payments, but I can't be sure of that."

"You've investigated many drug dealers, have you not?"

Cook nods. "I have."

"Do they generally kill their customers? Is that how they run their business?"

"They do not generally kill their customers. But it can happen."

"Thank you."

Judge Lockett tells us that he has docket issues to deal with tomorrow, so we will not be in session. It's welcome news; we need the time to deal with the Mullens situation.

I've already decided that I am going to call Sharon Keller to testify. It's not that I think the metaverse guys could have killed Rayburn; it's more that I need a delay to keep the defense case going until someway, somehow, I can get Mullens on the stand.

It is clear that we have a difficult task ahead of us.

Marcus and Corey have checked out the house that Sam believes Mullens is either hiding in or is being kept against his will.

Corey and Marcus agree with Sam, especially since not only is the house registered in the name of someone who we can't identify, but there are New Jersey plates on the two cars parked in front. They didn't see anyone go in or out, except to pick up a food delivery. And it wasn't Mullens.

So we need to figure out what to do. We have to get Mullens out of there; it's essential that we talk to him to discover what the hell is going on. But it is not going to be easy. The house is relatively isolated, with a lot of open space around it on all sides except the back, where there is a significant amount of woodland.

But even with Marcus on our side, we are not the US Marine Corps. We do not have equipment to storm that house; we can't use tear gas or tanks. We would be exposing ourselves to detection and failure.

And what if Mullens dies in the process; where are we then? And how would law enforcement treat us? We don't have a warrant; we can't just storm buildings because we think bad guys are in there.

And what if we're wrong in the first place? What if Sylvia and Harry Swathouse live there with Sylvia's parents? Maybe Sylvia is sick with the flu and no one else knows how to cook, so they keep ordering in. Maybe the food delivery people can't come to the house because Sylvia is contagious.

"We can't do this," I say to the team after detailing all the reasons. "This is not the Alamo. We need to turn this over to law enforcement."

Nobody disagrees with that assessment. "It would have to be local police up in Rockland. Or New York State Police," Laurie says, because the Jersey cops looking for Mullens would not have jurisdiction in Rockland County, since it's in New York.

I shake my head. "It has to be Homeland Security; they have an interest in this already and won't need educating. I'll contact the guy who was following me . . . Agent Bridges. I'll turn it over to him, with conditions. If he doesn't agree, then we go to the New York State Police."

We kick it around some more, but everybody agrees with my conclusion; there are just too many negatives attached to our storming the house ourselves. Even if we were successful, and with the quality of our group I think we would be, it still doesn't make sense.

It's almost ten o'clock when everyone leaves. I call Agent Bridges at the number he left me, but I get his voicemail. This is clearly his personal phone, so I leave a message that it is urgent he call me.

I head into the den to prepare for my examination of

Sharon Keller. I haven't given it much thought because I wasn't going to call her, but that's changed now.

As I'm going over the details, I play the video that we took the night we trapped the two guys at Dani Kendall's house.

Laurie: "That's not a convertible out there."

Bad guy: "Yeah, that's okay. A friend of ours is following with your car."

Laurie: "When?"

Bad guy: "When he gets here. You got the money?"

Laurie: "I've got it. But I want to see the car first."

Bad guy: "I told you it will be here. Where is the cash?"

Laurie: "It's not cash. It's a check."

Second bad guy: "This is bullshit."

Bad guy: "What are you trying to pull? It was supposed to be cash."

Laurie: "I know, but I wasn't comfortable getting all that cash. The check is good, but I don't like this."

Bad guy: "You're going to like this even less."

Laurie: "What are you doing? You need to leave now."

Bad guy: "If there's no cash, maybe you can pay us another way."

Laurie: "Or maybe not."

Bad guy: "What the hell?"

This portion ends with Marcus "neutralizing" the two men. I'm pleased that the video shows how dangerous the two guys are, threatening Laurie with the knife. The second part of the tape is later, when we questioned them about Rayburn.

Me: "Tell us about Steven Rayburn."

Bad guy: "Who?"

Me: "He's the professor who you met online and who hacked into your devices."

Bad guy: "That son of a bitch. He ruined my computer and two headsets. My computer guy can't figure out what is wrong."

Sam: "Can I get his computer? I want to take a look at it."

Me: "Is there anyone in your house tonight?"

Bad guy: "No."

Me: "Okay, let's get back to Rayburn. We know you killed him."

Bad guy: "He's dead? That's the best news I heard all day."

Me: "He threatened you, ruined your devices, and you didn't do anything? You just let him slide?"

Bad guy: "He was on our list."

Me: "Here's the way this is going to go down, losers. The cops are on their way, and you're going to take a big fall for this. Attempted robbery and assault with a deadly weapon. You're going to do hard time, with no avatars to lay it off on.

"If and when you get out, we will be watching you, online and in the real world. And if we see anything that

makes us come after you, you will wish you were back in prison."

Me (to Marcus): "After the cops pick up this garbage, can you take Sam to get that computer?"

The first part of the tape is very usable; it shows the two guys as dangerous in the way they threaten Laurie with the knife.

The second part, while more relevant to our case, is a mixed bag. It shows their hatred for Rayburn, which is the only reason I am bringing this whole situation before the jury. But their surprise at his being dead seems genuine; if the jury believes them, then they won't see them as the actual killers.

But a different part of the second tape interests me even more, and I call Sam to discuss it. He left here not long ago, so I'm sure he must still be in his car driving home.

"Talk to me," he says, which is the way he always answers his phone.

"Sam, do you still have the computer you got from the metaverse creep?"

"Yeah; it's frustrating as hell."

"You still can't get it to work?"

"It's worse than that. I also can't figure out what's wrong with it. There's got to be a virus, or malware, but I can't find it."

"Keep trying," I say, even though I now believe it's a waste of time.

"Oh, I will."

Five minutes after I get off the phone with Sam, Agent Bridges calls me back. "This better be good."

It doesn't feel like he is trying to establish a warm relationship with me. "I know where Mullens is."

"I'm listening."

"I assumed that. I'm willing to tell you, but on a couple of conditions."

"Don't screw with me, Carpenter."

"You know what, Bridges? You're a pain in the ass; I'm going to deal with a more accommodating law enforcement organization. People who appreciate me."

He sighs. "What are the conditions?"

"We extricate him tomorrow night is the first one. We immediately question him together is another. And the third one is that he testify in my trial if I want him to, which I will be able to decide after we question him."

"That would be up to him."

"I'm aware of that, and at this point I'm not sure if he's a prisoner or a coconspirator or both."

"Where is he?" Bridges asks.

"Notably absent so far from this conversation is you agreeing to my conditions."

"I'll call you back in fifteen minutes."

"Okay. But I should also tell you that I know what he and Rayburn were working on and why you want to intervene."

"Then why don't you tell me?"

"They were trying to develop a computer virus that absolutely cannot be detected. It would be invaluable to another country like, say, Russia. But you already know this, and we're just cutting into your fifteen minutes."

"I cannot confirm or deny that."

"I have no interest in your doing either," I say. "But there's one other thing you don't know."

"And that is?"

"Rayburn already accomplished it." I'm not positive about this, but if Sam can't detect a virus in the metaverse guy's computer, I'm betting it can't be detected. That's what made me think this is what is going on, and Bridges has by his silence confirmed it.

"How do you know that?" Bridges asks.

"I don't think I'm going to share that with you right now. But it gives us something to ask Mullens."

Bridges called back eight minutes after we got off the phone and agreed to meet me at our house this morning.

He wanted to do it at his office in Manhattan, but I insisted that we do it here. I have found that at meetings of this kind home-field advantage is important. I've also found that in the mornings I hate fighting the ridiculous traffic into the city.

He shows up promptly at nine o'clock with two other agents, who he introduces only by their last names, Ramirez and Coble. I have our whole team with me; Corey and Marcus are the ones who've seen the house, so after the agents look over the photographs, the two can answer any questions they have.

After Bridges again promised to honor my conditions, he had one of his own. "None of you can be on-site when we conduct this operation. There is too much chance of detection and danger to civilians, in this case, you."

I look at Corey and Marcus, who both nod slightly in agreement. "Okay," I say. "But then you will have to immediately bring Mullens to a location where we can question him, as per our agreement."

"It will be in one of our vans; that way it can be recorded."

"Fair enough."

Corey then becomes the spokesman for our side, first taking Bridges and the others through the reasons we believe Mullens is in that house. He glosses over getting into the LogMeIn and Chow Down computers, but doesn't gloss quite enough for Bridges not to notice.

"Did you get that information from these companies?"

"In a manner of speaking," I say. "Don't go there."

He nods his understanding; he has no interest in opening an investigation into illegal hacking.

Corey then shows the agents the photographs and describes the area in ways that still photographs just can't. The agents listen without interruption until he is finished, then ask a few questions about the wooded area behind the house. Corey and Marcus couldn't get good pictures of it, but Sam has gone on Google Maps and gotten overhead shots of it.

"And they order food every night from this service?" Bridges asks.

"Yes," Sam says. "Always between six and six thirty."

"That's our way in," Bridges says. "And we go through the back at the same time. I need to take all of this to our people. Our experts may have other ideas."

"Fine," I say.

"I'll call you this afternoon with a meeting location and time."

"Also fine."

"You'd better hope that Mullens is in there and it's not some random family watching *Wheel of Fortune.*"

"No, you're the one who should hope that," I say. "You're the one that will be in their living room. Maybe, just in case, you should be prepared to buy a vowel."

They leave and I find myself wishing that court was in session today, a wish I can never remember having before. But it would take my mind off the upcoming events tonight, which will probably decide the trial one way or the other.

So all I can do is further get ready to examine Sharon Keller. I can't prepare questions to ask Mullens on the stand until I know what he has to say tonight, and whether he'll be a hostile witness.

I'll also walk the dogs a lot and probably drive Laurie crazy. I do both of those things when I'm nervous, and when I'm not nervous.

Bridges calls at two o'clock to tell me where to wait for him and Mullens in the van. I ask him what the attack plan is, but he has no interest in telling me, which I understand.

That part of it is his show. My show is in court . . . hopefully.

Laurie and I are having maybe the weirdest dinner of our lives.

We are sitting in the Mount Ivy Diner on Route 202 in Pomona, less than five minutes from the house where we believe Samuel Mullens is. The plan, as Agent Bridges related it to me, is that once the operation is over, he will call me and tell me to come out to the parking lot.

The van will then pull up and Laurie and I will get in. We will then conduct an initial interview with Mullens, after which they will take him away. We'll find out during the interview if he will agree to testify, and if I will want him to. The latter, obviously, depends on what he has to say.

So here we sit, Laurie checking her phone for any news alerts about any large-scale police operations in Pomona, New York. There is always the chance that it is over and that Bridges and the other agents are having a beer somewhere; I have no mechanism to hold him to his promise.

At seven fifteen the phone rings. I answer and Bridges simply says, "We're on our way."

I haven't gotten the check yet, so I put down enough money to pay three times what it might be, and we go outside to the back of the parking lot, per the plan. Within three minutes two vehicles pull up, a large van and a dark blue sedan.

The van door opens; one of the agents who was with Bridges at our house this morning motions for me to come toward the van, and as we do so, Bridges gets out.

"It went perfectly," Bridges says. "Except for the two people who died in the shooting."

"They resisted?" I ask.

"Unfortunately."

"But Mullens is all right?"

"Fortunately. Get in; you can ask him yourself."

"Was I right about the undetectable virus?"

"Yes," Bridges says. Then, "Come on."

Laurie and I get in the van, and Mullens is sitting on a bench in the back. He looks pale and shaken; he's probably lost ten pounds since I saw him last. It's either from stress or Chow Down delivers awful food.

"Hello, Professor," I say, but he just nods in response.

"This is Laurie Collins. We're going to ask you a few questions."

Another nod; it doesn't seem to be a conversation he is looking forward to.

"How did you come to be a part of this?" I ask.

"I knew Nucci from being a consultant to his software company. He wanted me on the project, or so he said. But he really wanted Steven."

"Why?"

"I didn't know this at the time, but somehow the Russians found out that Steven was doing some groundbreaking work on viruses. I'm an expert on spyware, so they clearly thought they could get us together to get them what they wanted."

"So you knew from the beginning that the Russians were behind it?"

"No. I thought it was for Nucci's company."

Mullens may well be lying; he's a smart guy and he would likely know treason when he sees it, or when he commits it. But that doesn't interest me now.

"And Steven . . . Rayburn . . . finally succeeded in creating that virus?"

"Yes, but I'm the only one he told. He was in pretty bad shape with his addiction at that point, so he turned his work over to me and said he was leaving."

This is consistent with his telling the head of the department that his work was finished, and he was leaving Rutgers. "Where was he going?"

"I don't know; I'm not sure he knew. He wanted to get himself clean; the drug habit was starting to overwhelm him and he knew it."

I might as well ask the key question. "So that's why they killed him?"

Mullens shakes his head. "I don't know if they killed him or not. They never mentioned it, and I wasn't about to ask. But if they did, something must have happened between them; Steven could behave erratically. Maybe they decided he was a danger to them."

That was not on the list of the answers I wanted to hear. "So you never told them the work was accomplished?"

"No. I was afraid when they found out, they would want

to get rid of me. They . . . Borodin . . . the others . . . are extremely dangerous. They have no conscience. I was pretending to continue the work; I would tell them I was getting close and then would have a setback. I don't know how long I could have held them off. They were getting desperate. . . . What Steven created . . . it's like a cyber nuclear weapon."

"How did it work?" Bridges asks, entering the conversation for the first time.

"Viruses have a code, and they replicate themselves. Steven's creation rewrites its own code, over and over. There is no way to find it because it keeps changing; you don't know what you're looking for. That's the very simple explanation."

"Did Rayburn have any dealings with Nucci or Borodin that didn't include you?" I ask.

"Definitely. He was the one that was important to them; I was just a means to an end."

"So something could have happened to poison their relationship and you might not have known about it?"

Mullens shrugs. "I suppose it's possible, but Steven was my friend. I think he would have told me if it was anything important."

"Can you think of any reason why someone besides Nucci and Borodin would have wanted to smash Rayburn's computer?"

"No. And I knew his password, so I tried to access his work in the cloud. There must have been so much on there of value. But it was erased . . . he must have erased it. He even wrote over some of what was in the cloud."

"But he had already given his work on the virus over to you?"

"Yes."

I look at Laurie, but she signals that I've covered everything. I can always come back to him if I think of anything else, but for now that's it.

"Do you know how they found me?" Mullens asks.

"Through your LogMeIn account."

He smiles; the only smile I've seen out of him.

The conversation I had with Samuel Mullens was nowhere near satisfactory.

I had been counting on him to testify, but there is no way I can call him now. All I wanted was for him to say that Nucci and Borodin killed Rayburn, but he won't say it.

The things he said I have basically already conveyed to the jury. I've connected him to Nucci and Borodin, and I've informed them that he was missing and probably the victim of foul play.

All that he's added that I haven't gotten into the trial was that the Russians were behind it, but that doesn't get me anywhere. The link to bad guys has already been established; if those bad guys are Nucci and Borodin, or the Russians, or both, it doesn't matter.

In the jurors' eyes, bad guys are bad guys.

But if Mullens gets on the stand and implicates these guys in everything except the Rayburn killing, it would be devastating to my case. The jury would obviously see that he is not protecting them and in fact has a reason to want to bury them.

In such a circumstance, if he still won't say definitively

that they committed the murder, it will undo a lot of the good that we've accomplished.

I could call Agent Bridges to testify, but that doesn't get me any further than using Mullens. Bridges would, in his position with Homeland Security, add some gravitas to the proceedings, but he would still have to relate that Mullens does not know who killed Rayburn.

Hopefully I've established Nucci and Borodin as credible alternative killers, but as is always the case with trials and juries, I'm not going to know until I know.

In the meantime, I'm going to put Sharon Keller on the stand and bring the jury into the metaverse, as it relates to this trial. I risk the "throwing things against the wall to see if something sticks" situation, but I think the positives outweigh the negatives.

The two metaverse guys are dangerous and credible as killers. They had a huge grudge and desire for revenge against Rayburn, so bringing them in is useful. Hopefully they will stick against that wall.

After that I will have used all the bullets in my gun. I will have shown Rayburn to be associated with any number of people all recognized by law enforcement as dangerous.

Nabers only has Brian Bremer, who had until now never been accused of anything in his entire, young life. Unfortunately, Nabers also has Brian at the murder scene, with the victim's blood on him, and that victim's possessions in Brian's apartment.

So as evidence goes, I have quantity and Nabers has quality.

Sharon Keller is obviously nervous when she takes the stand.

I tried to tell her that it's not going to be an ordeal, that we are going to have a conversation like we had in my office. There is no chance she believed me, plus I think she knows that, unlike in my office, our conversation is going to be followed by a cross-examination.

I ask a bunch of questions about her background, where she lives, how many siblings she has, and so forth, not because they are in any way relevant, but just to calm her down and get her to focus. It seems to work; she even smiles a couple of times.

"Do you spend a lot of time on the computer?" I ask. "I don't mean for work; I mean for fun, recreationally."

She smiles again. "More than I should."

"Did you ever enter something called the metaverse?"

"I used to fairly frequently."

She launches into a brief description of what the metaverse is and what it's like to be in there. I then ask the judge if I can play a short video to illustrate what she's been talking about, and he allows it.

I hope the jury understands it; these do not seem like the kind of people you'd run into in your neighborhood metaverse.

When the video is finished, I say, "When I asked you earlier if you had ever entered the metaverse, you said, 'I used to fairly frequently.' You don't anymore?"

"I try not to."

"Why is that?"

"I had a bad experience, a very upsetting experience."

I ask her to describe it. She starts with "It's hard for some people to understand, but I was sexually assaulted."

"Physically? Or online? Are you saying your avatar was assaulted?"

She nods. "It was as if it was happening to me, like it was a terrible dream that was real at the same time. But I couldn't wake up because I was already awake, and I had to watch. I panicked and I couldn't get away."

I introduce for the record a story about the same thing happening to a woman in England, and how the attackers are being prosecuted for the crime.

"What were the names of your attackers?"

"I only know their online names. They were X-er, and Shan-man and Ta-al Dude. I think he meant 'tall dude,' but for some reason there was a hyphen between *ta* and *al.*"

"The names were written on the screen?"

"Yes, and also spoken."

"Did you know Professor Steven Rayburn?"

She nods. "I did. I met Steven in the metaverse. He was very nice to me."

"Did he see what happened to you?"

"Yes. He helped to stop it, and then he told me that he was going to punish the people that did it."

"So you continued to talk to him online?"

"Yes, we went into a private space; you can do that."

"Did he punish them?"

She describes how he was able to identify two of them, X-er and Shan-man, and said he was going to destroy their devices. "Then, about a week later, he told me he did it."

Sharon has been a sympathetic witness, and Nabers handles her with kid gloves, especially because she has not said anything to damage his case.

He lets her off the stand and I call Laurie as my next witness. I let her describe her career as a police officer and as my investigator. She also says that we are married, just in case the jury should find out and think we were trying to hide something.

I then use my questions to get her to describe the online scam we pulled to draw the two guys to the house she was occupying, though she does not reveal that it was Dani Kendall's house.

"They were supposed to be bringing me a used car, a convertible, and I had agreed to pay them seventeen thousand dollars in cash. They showed up in one car, which was not a convertible."

Judge Lockett lets me play the video of that night, which shows them threatening Laurie with the knife and preparing to attack her. I am obligated to play it straight through, so while they said they were furious at Rayburn and he was "on our list" for destroying their devices, they also claimed not to have known he was dead.

They also said that their "computer guy" couldn't figure out what was wrong with their devices, just as Sam couldn't when he got their computers.

Overall the tape is a mixed bag; I have to hope that jurors will believe that two obvious slimeballs could be lying when they denied killing Rayburn.

The problem is that even I believed them.

My next witness is the recalling of Adam Lusk, who was also a prosecution witness.

I reestablish that he was Rayburn's assistant and then start off by asking what Rayburn was like. "You spent a lot of time with him?"

"I did. I had a dual purpose: to assist him in whatever he needed in terms of his work, and to learn from him in the process. He was brilliant."

"Would you say he was a nice man?"

"I would, definitely. He had his moments, but everyone does."

"Did you two ever argue?"

"Of course. He was very opinionated, and so am I. We argued at least once a day, maybe more."

"You testified that you witnessed the argument in class between Brian Bremer and Rayburn. Is that right?"

"Yes."

"But you did not think it was serious?"

Lusk nods. "Correct."

"Were any of your arguments as heated as the one he had with Mr. Bremer?"

"More so."

"Ever violent?" I ask.

"Of course not."

"Did you see him after class the day he and Mr. Bremer argued?"

"Yes. For a couple of hours."

"Was he furious about it?"

Lusk shakes his head. "Not at all. He never mentioned it."

"You said you were involved with his work, is that right?"

"Yes."

"All of it?"

"Except for one project. He was very secretive about it."

"Is that the one on which he was collaborating with Professor Mullens?"

"Yes."

"Was he working on it for Thomas Nucci?"

"I couldn't say."

"Did your closeness extend to joining him when he entered the metaverse?" I ask.

"No, I should have said . . . that's the other thing he was secretive about. But that wasn't a source of contention between us because it wasn't work related, and I had no interest in it. I've never done it myself."

"So if he was upset or worried about something connected to that metaverse, he would not have confided it to you?"

"Probably not."

I let Lusk off the stand and Nabers has only a few

perfunctory questions for him. My last witness is Mark Abrams, BJ's friend from school.

I'm not going to spend much time with him; he's there to reinforce what Lusk just said and give an additional character reference.

After setting him up, I ask, "So you were in the class the day Mr. Bremer and Professor Rayburn argued about his test grade?"

Abrams nods. "Yeah . . . yes. It was nothing. I mean, if it wasn't for what happened afterwards with people talking about it, I would have forgotten."

"So you didn't worry your friend would turn violent?"

"BJ? I mean, Brian? No chance."

"You never saw him act violently?"

"I never even saw him angry. He's like the most mellow guy I know."

"Did you ever go into the metaverse?"

"Me? Yeah, a bunch of times. We all do."

"Did you ever encounter Professor Rayburn in there?"

Abrams shakes his head. "No. Never. At least, I don't think so."

I'm finished with my questions and Nabers doesn't even bother cross-examining.

Then I say the five words that rank in scariness with "I've reviewed your biopsy results."

"Your Honor, the defense rests."

Resting a case is like skydiving.

You can do everything to prepare for your jump. You can pack and repack your parachute, you can make sure you're at the right altitude, you can jump smoothly out of the plane without getting caught on anything, and you can confirm in advance that the area below is conducive to a safe landing.

But once you leave the plane, if something goes wrong, if that parachute doesn't open, there's not a damn thing you can do about it. And once you've presented all your evidence in a trial, you're in the same boat.

Or plane.

That's why I don't like to jump out of planes, and I don't like to try cases.

Of course, we still have the closing arguments, but all they do is summarize and make the case we have already made. At best they can cement the leanings that the jurors already have, but I strongly doubt that they change minds.

In this trial, the closing argument is more important for the defense than the prosecution. That's because the prosecution case is completely straightforward; there is nothing confusing about it. Our side is the opposite of that; the jurors must be prepared to make connections and attach significance to them.

I would feel better if there weren't questions that I can't answer, the main one being why Nucci and Borodin would kill Rayburn.

The only thing I can think of is that Rayburn found out that the work he was doing was actually for the Russians, and he was preparing to sabotage their efforts and go to the US authorities. That would have blown the whole thing up, so even though Rayburn was incredibly valuable to them, they would have had to get rid of him.

Laurie points out something else to me: we now have to worry about Borodin seeking revenge against none other than Andy Carpenter. In his eyes I have single-handedly destroyed everything he had worked for.

I don't know him that well, but I don't think he's the type to shrug and say, "You got me this time . . . good on you."

We had taken some comfort in that they would not want to do anything to call even more attention to the trial and to their conspiracy. That's now out the window; Homeland Security has blown it up and has Rayburn's work.

There were three men with Mullens in the house in Pomona. Two of them died in the shoot-out and the other is in custody. Unfortunately, none of them are Borodin.

Of course, by now Borodin could be back in Russia. His work here ended, albeit unsuccessfully, so I'm hoping he's been exiled to a gulag. But if he's here, he could be a problem. He's not exactly a guy who fears danger; he even threatened Marcus.

"Marcus is looking for him," Laurie says.

"As is the entire US government."

She smiles. "My money is on Marcus."

"What's he doing?"

"He's going to some of Nucci's people, who at this point hate the Russians for killing Nucci and for forcing them out. He wants them to tell him where the Russians hang out."

"I'm sure the Feds know all that; Borodin is not just hanging out there doing vodka shots with his buddies."

"Right. But Marcus plans to convince one of them to reveal where Borodin is hiding. Marcus can convince people in the way the Feds can't."

I would never doubt Marcus, but I can't say that I'm confident he'll find Borodin. Meanwhile, Laurie still has the two ex-cops watching me and our house.

I've asked Agent Bridges to inform me if he gets any information on Borodin's whereabouts, and he's promised to do so. Certainly they have a strong interest in capturing him, which might be enough to make him leave the area. And Bridges understands that I'm at risk.

But I can't worry about Borodin now, even though I'll certainly continue to worry about him. I have to give the closing statement and then worry about the jury.

Borodin scares me, but at this moment the jury scares me more.

"Ladies and gentlemen, it isn't often that I get a prediction correct," Nabers says.

"I'm going on my tenth consecutive year of predicting that the Knicks will win the NBA championship. But I made a prediction about this trial, and it was one hundred percent accurate, so I hope you'll forgive me if I savor it.

"I stood here at the beginning of the trial, and I know that feels to you like a very long time ago, and I told you that we would present a series of facts to prove, beyond a reasonable doubt, that Brian Bremer brutally murdered Professor Steven Rayburn.

"So let's recap, starting with the motive. They argued; everyone in the class saw it. It doesn't matter that Adam Lusk and Mark Abrams and the other students might not have thought it was a big deal.

"All that matters is how Brian Bremer and Steven Rayburn felt about it. And then we found out that Steven Rayburn was apparently contemplating disciplinary action against a student, soon after the argument took place. Is it reasonable to assume that it was against the student that had just threatened his authority?

"And is it also reasonable to believe that Brian Bremer, in his unstable mind, wanted to protect himself from that discipline and wanted revenge against the person who would impose it?

"Yes, both are reasonable conclusions. But if that's the only incriminating evidence that existed, you would not be sitting here and I would not be talking to you.

"Mr. Bremer was standing over the body when the police arrived. What was he doing there? Did Mr. Carpenter present any evidence that they had a meeting scheduled? A meeting that would have been in violation of university rules?

"So was it a coincidence that the man who argued with Professor Rayburn happened to be the one standing over his body? Of course not. But suppose you still wanted to give Mr. Bremer the benefit of the doubt. Maybe he was the world's unluckiest person, caught in a classic case of 'wrong place, wrong time.'

"Then there is the little matter of the victim's watch and money in his apartment. That pushes it over the line; no one is that unlucky.

"Mr. Carpenter would have you believe that the killer was Thomas Nucci, or Gregori Borodin, or Al Capone, or Osama bin Laden. He'll blame anyone he can find, but you know what? None of those people were standing over the body, the victim's blood on them, and the victim's possessions in their apartment.

"You do not have to have seen Mr. Bremer smash Steven Rayburn over the head. Very few crimes are solved by eyewitnesses seeing them as they took place. People tend to commit crimes, like murder, when no one is around to observe them.

"So I'll ask you to please do what I asked of you in my opening statement. Please follow the facts.

"Thank you very much for your dedicated service."

Unlike Nabers, who sits at a lectern and often checks his notes, I walk around and basically wing it. I know what I am going to say, I just don't know how I am going to say it until it comes out.

"Ladies and gentlemen, Thomas Nucci and Gregori Borodin are two names who Mr. Nabers would have you believe I just picked out of the air. But here is a fact that is beyond dispute: they paid James Howarth to become Mr. Bremer's lawyer.

"And lest you think they were doing it out of a real concern for Mr. Bremer, they told Mr. Howarth to get him to plead guilty. Failing that, he was supposed to ensure that he was convicted by a jury like you.

"Try and imagine why they did that. Is it possible that they were responsible for the murder themselves and knew that once Mr. Bremer was put away, without significant investigation, they would be in the clear? Can you think of another reason that makes sense?

"And once Nucci and Borodin were in the picture, look who else joined in that picture. Professor Samuel Mullens, a consultant to Nucci's company who was working on a project with Professor Rayburn, and who wound up kidnapped. Then there was Rufus Aronde, Rayburn's drug dealer, who was also in the employ of Nucci, and who also wound up missing. James Howarth, by the way, is also missing. It seems like every person that connected Rayburn to Thomas Nucci and Gregori Borodin is mysteriously missing, or worse.

"Then, to top it all off, we have the two thugs that Rayburn met in his secret life in the metaverse, both of whom swore revenge against him. These are men who you saw on tape threaten a woman with a knife. . . . Who knows what they would have done to her?

"I'm going to admit something: at this point I simply don't know what Professor Rayburn did to earn a spot on the list of people that Nucci and Borodin either killed or made disappear. Maybe he realized that the work he was doing was going to wind up in Russian hands, and he could not stomach becoming a traitor. Maybe they found out he was going to go to the police. Or maybe he had finished what he was doing for them and was therefore no longer useful.

"Someday we might find out. But there are some things we do know. We know that Rayburn had many connections to people that were killers. We know that those people had ample resources and the ability to frame Brian Bremer for the murder.

"We also know that Brian has absolutely no history of violence or criminality. None. Mr. Nabers would have you believe that someone who has lived an exemplary life suddenly, because of a minor dispute over a grade, brutally smashed a man over the head, killing him.

"You may not agree with everything I've said, but I would submit that you cannot be positive I am wrong. You cannot think I am wrong beyond a reasonable doubt.

"And if that is the case, you cannot convict Brian Bremer.

"Please give this young man his life back."

I go back to the defense table and pat BJ on the shoulder, and I look at Doris Bremer, as always in the front row, who is giving me the thumbs-up. I don't mention to either of them that if I had taken Borodin's deal, BJ might already have his life back.

Every time a jury starts their deliberation, I ask myself if we're better off if they're out a long or short time. Since I am basically a negative person, I usually decide that a short deliberation is bad for us, and a long one is bad for us.

Most normal lawyers in my position would probably be rooting for the jury to be out a long time. That's because the prosecution position is simple, based on simple facts. If the jury buys those facts, then there isn't that much to talk about.

Our defense case requires more analysis, more weighing of possibilities. That takes a bit longer.

Of course most defense lawyers would be hoping for a hung jury. I know that is far better than a conviction, but it's not something I root for. I want to win, not tie. A tie means BJ stays in jail for a long time waiting for a retrial.

It's now been a day and a half since the judge gave the jury their charge and sent them off. They are sequestered while deliberating so I can't even fly a plane overhead with a banner saying FREE BJ. All I can do is wait.

When I'm stressed, I walk the dogs way too much, so during jury verdicts Tara and Hunter cringe every time I pick up the leash. Laurie tells me that the exercise bike would be a good way to reduce my stress level, but that is not going to happen.

At 6:00 P.M. I get a call from the court clerk telling me that the jury has concluded their work for the day, so we won't be getting a verdict until tomorrow at the earliest.

That sends me on another dog walk; I think Tara and Hunter are going to go on a sit-down strike. But they stagger along with me; Tara has probably told Hunter about the verdict-waiting lunacy, since she has been through it for a much longer time.

When I get back, the phone is ringing, and I hear Laurie answer it in the kitchen. She comes toward the front door, the phone in her hand, and says, "Marcus thinks he knows where Borodin is."

"Where?"

She talks back into the phone. "Marcus, what's the address?" As she is talking, she walks over to a desk and writes down what he is saying. "Got it." Then she turns to me, "What should I tell him?"

"He should not do anything. I will call Bridges."

"Marcus, don't do anything. Andy is going to call Bridges." Then, "Marcus . . ."

She turns to me. "He hung up; I think he's going there."

"Where is it?"

She hands me the piece of paper; it's an address in Little Falls, about fifteen minutes from here. "You call Corey and I'll call Bridges," I say. "Let's do it on the way."

Laurie is already on her cell, calling Corey and updating him on the situation. Once we get in the car and are on the way, I call Bridges and get his voicemail, so I leave a detailed message, including the address. If need be, when we get there, I can call local or state police.

"Did Marcus say what he was going to do?" I ask.

"I hope he's only going to confirm that Borodin is there, from a distance."

"I don't think so."

"Why not?" she asks.

"Because Borodin threatened him, and because he's Marcus."

I had no idea what we were going to find when we got to the Little Falls address, but it certainly was not this.

This is surreal.

There is a small house, isolated with no other houses around. It might even be a farmhouse; it's hard to tell in the darkness. Marcus's car is there and we can see the front of the house from where we are.

It's hard to make out, but there are two men in front of the house, facing off against each other. I think one is Marcus and the other one, significantly larger, is probably Borodin.

"Pull up," Laurie says, and I can already see the gun in her hand. "No reason to sneak up now; too late for that."

So we drive forward, until we're maybe thirty yards away. I put on the bright headlights and I can make things out more clearly. In addition to the two men standing, a third man is lying on the ground, unmoving. I'm assuming he was a bodyguard for Borodin, maybe stationed outside to protect against people like Marcus.

Nobody protects against people like Marcus.

"Let's go," Laurie says, and she is out of the car and running toward the action. I'm slower to get out of the car and I walk rather than run because I am not Laurie, I am Andy Carpenter.

I expect Laurie, who is already pointing her gun, to scream that Borodin should put his hands up, that it's all over. But she doesn't; I don't think she wants to deprive Marcus of his moment.

I see an object on the ground, shining in the light of the car beams. It looks like a gun; maybe the bodyguard had it and Marcus had decided he should no longer have it.

Borodin and Marcus are acting as if we are not even there, and on some level I wish we weren't. Borodin is slowly circling him, actually smiling, seeming to relish what is about to happen. Marcus only turns slightly to keep him in his sight and is otherwise unmoving.

From experience, I know that the only time Marcus is more dangerous than when he is unmoving is when he is moving.

Suddenly, Borodin strikes, but with his feet. He goes after Marcus with what looks like a martial arts kick. It surprises me; Borodin is the bigger man and I would have thought he would try to use that to his advantage.

Marcus takes the kick in the shoulder and is moved back slightly by it. Probably wanting to take advantage of a good strategy, Borodin throws another kick with the same leg.

Big mistake.

Marcus intercepts and grabs the leg and lifts it as high as he can, causing Borodin to land on the ground on his back. Marcus then grabs Borodin's left arm, turning it and then bringing his knee down on the elbow.

It bends it in a direction that elbows are not supposed to bend and causes Borodin to scream; if I have ever heard a scream that loud, I can't remember when. That arm is going to be useless from now on, unless Borodin wants to use it as a hood ornament.

Marcus, maybe in an attempt to get Borodin to stop the annoying screaming, kicks him in the side of the head, and he goes silent.

I don't think Borodin is going to come out for round two.

Laurie is still holding the gun from her vantage point on the left side. The gun on the ground is between the two unconscious men on the right side, so Laurie yells to me to kick it out of the way.

Kicking guns is within my skill set, so I go to do so. Just as I swing my leg, Borodin suddenly and violently springs into action. He grabs me with his good right arm and pulls himself erect.

The next thing I know, he is standing behind me, his right arm around my throat. He talks to Laurie and Marcus. "You make one move, one move at all, and I will break this asshole's neck."

I'm the asshole he is talking about, and it is a fair description of me for letting myself get put into this situation. And the neck breaking seems realistic; already the pressure on it is so severe I'm having trouble breathing.

I am scared to death; I am afraid he is killing me without his even trying to kill me.

"Let him go," Laurie screams, still pointing the gun. But there is no way she can shoot; I am directly in front of Borodin. Marcus, for his part, hasn't said anything.

I'm starting to gag; I'm in big trouble here.

"Let's get that gun," Borodin says, and he starts to move me toward the gun on the ground.

As we move slowly, shuffling sideways, I see that his left arm is hanging loosely at his side. I don't think he could move it if he wanted to; and it must hurt like hell.

I don't have much time left, so I do the only thing I can think of. I take my left hand, which has been trying without success to pry Borodin's arm off my neck, and bring it down on his ruined left elbow.

He lets out another horrible scream, and I'm able to move forward a few inches, but not enough to get away. There is a deafening sound in the night air, and my head and neck are suddenly wet.

Borodin lets me go and falls to the ground, and I look and see Corey, well off to the right side, gun in his hand. He's just shot Borodin in the head, which means the wet I am covered with is probably a combination of blood, skull, and brains.

It is without question the most disgusting experience I have ever had, and there is nothing in second place.

It was almost two in the morning when we finally got home.

Bridges and his people showed up fifteen minutes after Borodin's demise, and we were answering questions and giving statements for hours. I also thanked Corey four or five hundred times.

"You could have missed and hit me," I said.

He smiled. "That was a chance I was willing to take."

Bridges was not pleased that Borodin's head was blown off; it makes it much harder to interrogate him. But he did recognize that we, or actually Marcus, were able to find Borodin when the government could not.

At home I finally got into a hot shower to clean off the disgusting stuff; my plan was to stay in the shower until July 4. But I actually only stayed in for about twenty minutes; I was exhausted and needed to get to sleep.

Before I did so, I went in and hugged the sleeping Ricky; there was a time last night when I thought I might never get to do that again. Next I hugged Tara, Hunter, and Sebastian; the latter was annoyed that I woke him without also giving him a biscuit.

Just before we went to sleep, Laurie, who had been

unusually quiet, said, "Andy, I'm sorry. I never should have put you in that position."

"It was not your fault. I should have been more careful."

"You're not used to these situations. I should have realized that."

"Really, it's fine. I was trained for it; it reminded me of a final I took in law school."

She smiled. "That was great that you hit his elbow like that. Really smart."

"I'm just glad Corey is a good shot."

"So am I. I would dread having to start dating again."

I could have slept for a month, but Tara and her team had other ideas. For some reason they insist on eating and walking and are uninterested in the violence of the previous night. They didn't sign on for that when they agreed to live with a lawyer.

So the next morning we go for a long walk in Eastside Park, which lets me clear my head. I don't want to think about the case because I can no longer influence it. But I can't help it; I've been focused on it 24-7 for a long time, and I just can't turn it off.

For the most part, justice has been served and all the bad guys have received their due. Nucci and Borodin are dead. Aronde the drug dealer and James Howarth are missing and likely dead. I'm not sure whether Mullens knew what he was doing was wrong, but that will hopefully be determined one day.

But by any measure, the murder of Steven Rayburn has been avenged. Even the two metaverse guys are in prison for a long time.

The elephant in the park, of course, is BJ. If he gets convicted of the murder, then justice will be trashed. Worse yet, I will be the trasher, and BJ will be the trashee. That's because I will know until the day I die, which was almost last night, that I could have made a deal that would probably have freed him.

I go home and turn on the television. It's midmorning on a weekday, so no sports are on, and the news is unlikely to cheer me up, especially since the media is covering what happened last night.

I turn on a rerun of *Who Wants to Be a Millionaire* with Regis Philbin. I find it interesting that I actually care whether the contestants win or lose, even though it's more than twenty years ago and all the money has probably been spent ten times over.

The phone rings and I know what it is with absolute certainty, even before I see the caller ID. It's the court clerk, Rita Gordon. I once had an affair with Rita, at a time when Laurie and I were not yet together, that lasted about forty-five minutes. But they were forty-five great minutes.

"Andy, I heard you had quite a night last night. You're a hero."

"Just another day at the office."

She laughs. "Right. Okay, hero, get your ass down here. There's a verdict."

Laurie drives me down to the courthouse.

If I tried to drive myself, I would be so distracted that I'd wind up in the hospital, although I have to admit that the hospital is more appealing than the courthouse at this moment.

There is a big crowd, which has spilled out into the street. I don't think there is anything more dramatic in real life than a courtroom verdict when a lot is at stake, and apparently the citizens of Middlesex County feel the same way, because they are out in force.

Laurie parks in the back and we go in through the rear door and straight to the courtroom; Eddie is already at the defense table. BJ has not yet been brought in, but Doris Bremer sits in her front-row seat, where she has been throughout. She makes a crossing-fingers motion to me, and I try to manage a smile in return.

Nabers and his team are already at their table. Our eyes meet and he nods; I have no idea what he is thinking and I truthfully don't give a shit. I don't even care what the jury is thinking, because their thinking time is over. They have made a decision and committed it to paper, and it's too late for anyone to do anything about it.

BJ is brought in and says, "I've never been so nervous in my life." Usually the first words from a person in his position are "What do you think?" I suspect that he doesn't ask that because he can tell from my face what I think.

Actually, I have no idea what I think. I just want it to be over.

But it can't be over until the judge comes in, and that takes another ten excruciating minutes. I cannot imagine what he could be doing that is more important than this.

But he finally enters and we all rise. He cautions everyone that there is to be decorum in his courtroom after the verdict is announced. It's basically an empty threat; there's nothing he will actually do to anyone who screams with pleasure or disapproval, one way or the other.

The jury is brought in. I don't look at their faces because in the past that has been an inexact predictor, at least for me. Of course, if they have found BJ guilty, I will punch every one of them in the face, so I'll see them then.

The judge says a few more interminable things; he might as well be babbling because I don't hear or understand a single word he says. The only words I am interested in hearing are Rita Gordon's when she reads the verdict.

And finally it comes to that. The jury hands the verdict slip to the bailiff, who brings it to the judge, who directs that it be given to the court clerk, who is to read it. He directs BJ to stand, and he, Eddie, and I stand as one. I have my right hand on BJ's shoulder and Eddie has his left hand on the other shoulder.

I swear Rita looks at the paper and quickly glances at

me. I can't tell what that means because her expression reveals nothing, but I do believe she is rooting for me.

And then come the words:

"'We the jury, in the case of *New Jersey versus Brian Bremer,* as to count one, the homicide of Mr. Steven Rayburn, find the defendant, Brian Bremer, not guilty of the crime of first-degree homicide.'"

The courtroom erupts, prompting a lot of gavel-pounding. Brian hugs me, grabbing my neck so hard that it reminds me of Borodin. Then he turns and does the same to Eddie, who can probably handle it better.

I turn and look at Doris Bremer. If I've ever seen more joy on a face, I can't remember when. Not even Eli Manning's when he beat the Patriots.

Judge Lockett is still pounding his gavel, though the courtroom has gotten much quieter.

BJ leans over to me and says softly, "Of all the lawyers Murphy could have chosen, I'm glad he picked you."

Judge Lockett dismisses the jury with his thanks, says a few words to BJ, wishing him luck, and then adjourns the session.

They take BJ off to do some paperwork, and Laurie, Eddie, and I wait for him. Doris says that she'll meet us outside.

It's almost a half hour until we get out there; it's cold and cloudy out, but I can tell it feels like the best day ever for BJ when he gets outside in the fresh air.

There, at the bottom of the steps, is Doris Bremer and a friend. And also a second friend, who happens to be

Murphy. Apparently she had the friend wait outside with him; that's how confident she was of victory.

BJ runs down to Murphy, and some serious petting and rolling on the cement ensues.

Justice has been served.

Professor Samuel Mullens is apparently off the legal hook. I asked Agent Bridges if Mullens was going to be charged, and he said it was unlikely.

I would imagine there are two reasons for this. One is that there is no way to prove what he knew and when he knew it; what he did was only illegal if he knew he was doing it for the Russians. That they kidnapped him lends credence to the theory that he wasn't a knowing member of the conspiracy.

The other reason is likely that the US government does not want any public focus on the conspiracy because it does not want anyone to know about Rayburn's successful work on preventing virus detection. Bridges already told me that the whole thing was classified and gently threatened me with untold pain should I speak about it.

I'm okay with Mullens getting off. In legal terms, I could not prove beyond a reasonable doubt that he is guilty. I can't even say for sure that Rayburn was innocent; there's just no way to know.

And at this point, I don't care. I'm just glad it's over.

Tonight is our traditional victory party. It's more subdued this year, probably because it's not at Charlie's, which is our usual venue. Doris Bremer asked me if we could have it at her house. I was hesitant until she told me she would bake for the occasion.

So Laurie called a caterer and had dinner brought in, and I've brought Ricky, Tara, and Hunter, all of whom are close friends of the guest of honor, Murphy Bremer.

Also here are Marcus, Sam, Eddie, Corey, Simon Garfunkel, and Dani Kendall, Corey's girlfriend. Actually she has just recently become his fiancée, so that's another thing for us to celebrate. Edna couldn't make it; she's exhausted from working on the case.

There is little talk about the case; we've all lived it, and that's quite enough, thank you. We do update BJ on what happened that last night with Borodin. I try to make myself sound heroic, but I don't think he buys it, and most of the rest of the group were there, so they certainly don't buy it.

Laurie gently reprimands Marcus for disregarding her instructions and going to Borodin on his own. "Gently" is the only way to reprimand Marcus, but he seems unmoved and definitely unrepentant. I suspect he had a great time and our arrival only spoiled the fun.

BJ is going to go back to school right away. The head of the department, Jessica Kauffman, has told him they will make arrangements to allow him to catch up on the work he's missed. And he will of course keep his tuition scholarship.

Once he says this, Laurie correctly believes that it's the right time to make an announcement.

"The Andy and Laurie Carpenter scholarship fund has

gotten BJ a new apartment, nicer than the old one by a good deal." She turns to BJ. "It will be rent-free for as long as you are in school. We'll go down there with you to get the keys and help you set it up. The furniture will be arriving tomorrow."

"That's unbelievable," BJ says. "I can't thank you enough."

"She hasn't gotten to the best part yet," I say, and I turn it back to Laurie.

She smiles broadly. "They allow dogs."

Laurie didn't put this apartment thing for BJ together overnight.

It had been her idea, and I told her that if we won the case, we'd go ahead with it, but not to do anything until the trial was over.

She proceeded without waiting for a verdict because she was that confident we'd prevail, and because she's okay disregarding my requests. The reason she didn't tell me what she was doing was because I would say she was jinxing us . . . which I would have.

Laurie has learned to deal with my idiosyncrasies, which means basically to ignore them. I wish I could; it would make my life easier.

So we're down here with BJ and Doris and, of course, Murphy, helping them set things up. The apartment is right near campus, apparently much closer than BJ's previous place.

BJ has gone off to meet his friend Mark Abrams, and the two of them will be transporting BJ's things from the old apartment to this one. They said there's not a lot of stuff, mostly clothes and a computer and other incidentals.

The furniture arrives right on time, and Laurie and Doris

tell the deliverers where all the pieces go. I'm amazed that Laurie had the time to do all of this. She's amazing when she sets her mind to something.

This is a really nice apartment, certainly far nicer than anything I had in college. Laurie even ordered a large flat-screen, smart TV; it's lucky she knows how to set it up, because I wouldn't have a clue.

The apartment is also huge; Laurie went nuts on this one. It has a living room, kitchen, bedroom, and an office for BJ, I guess to study in. His office is nicer than mine; if we set fire to it, it would still be nicer than mine. And it's not above a fruit stand.

Murphy seems at home here already; he's found the dog bed that Doris brought with her and is sacked out in it.

After a couple of hours, BJ and Mark Abrams arrive with his stuff. They spend time unloading it all and bringing it in; I even help them to demonstrate my usefulness.

After we're done, BJ says, "This place is amazing. There is no way I can thank you."

"Do well in school," Laurie says.

Mark, meanwhile, is looking around and goes into the office. "Wow, you can even see the quad from here. I've gotta move in with you. I'll sleep here in the office."

Something about what he says jars me, but I can't figure out why. We say our good-byes, receiving repeated additional but unnecessary thank-yous from Doris and BJ.

Not until we're back in the car, stuck in traffic on the Garden State Parkway, do I realize why Mark's comment struck me the way it did.

And why it will cause me to do what I am about to do.

The person I need to talk to in order to test my theory is Adam Lusk.

He was surprised to hear from me again, but I told him I needed his help to wrap up something on the case, which was and is true.

We're not meeting in the student center this time, which since school is in session is likely to be crowded. I cleared using Rayburn's office as our meeting spot with Jessica Kauffman, the head of the department. She was happy to do it, also thanking me for proving BJ's innocence.

Lusk is already in the office when I arrive, and I close the door behind me. "Thanks for coming," I say.

"No problem. You did a great job for Brian. I knew you would; I told you I've followed your career."

I nod. "I remember. You almost went to law school."

He smiles. "Right."

"It's not too late. Maybe you can be one of those jailhouse lawyers."

"What are you talking about?" he asks, suddenly wary.

"One of those inmates who studies law books in the prison library, you know, always looking for a loophole that would allow for an appeal. You hear about those people—"

He stops me; obviously that's not what he meant by the question. "Why would I be an inmate? Why the hell would I be an inmate?"

"Duh," I say, to show that the answer should be obvious. "For killing Steven Rayburn. For smashing him over the head with a statue. I've got to admit, you almost got away with it."

"You're crazy."

"No, but I'll admit I'm a little slow. I should have picked up on it earlier. And it's the craziest thing; you know what made me realize it? The 'quad.'"

"What the hell does that mean?"

"The third person that Sharon ran into on the metaverse called a meeting area the quad. She had never heard that term used there before, but you used it, because you are a student here."

"You cannot prove any of this because it never happened."

"Wrong again. It turns out that you are the third guy who attacked her online. And you know how I know? Because your online name is Ta-al Dude. The *TA* is 'teacher's assistant,' because that's what you are, and the *AL* is 'Adam Lusk.' If you were going to commit a crime like that, you should have been more creative in coming up with a name.

"In fact, you said on the witness stand that you never were on the metaverse. They could charge you with perjury, but when they already have you for murder, the perjury charge will probably seem silly and unnecessary."

He stands up. "I'm getting out of here."

"No, you're not."

"You think you can stop me?"

"Probably not, but Marcus definitely can. Marcus?"

The door opens and Marcus is standing there.

"The police will be here soon," I say. "They're executing a search warrant on your apartment even as we speak. In the meantime, I thought you might want a list of the reasons I know you did it.

"The first time we met, you told me that you were never present when Rayburn was in the metaverse, except for a few seconds when you walked in on him. You said he kept it a secret from you. You also told me that you were never on it yourself, yet you knew he used his real name there. How would you know that?"

Lusk doesn't say anything.

"Never mind; I don't expect you to answer. It's okay, I'm on a roll. You had access to the keys to Brian's apartment because he told me he always left them in his coat outside the classroom. You had no trouble copying them. You were a TA; you could walk in and out of class. That's how you were able to get into his apartment to leave the watch and cash.

"And you witnessed the argument, which was why you chose him to be set up. Plus, you had access to a university phone, which is how you called him and pretended to be the clerk telling him to go to Rayburn's house at a precise time.

"Rayburn didn't just identify only two of the three people that attacked Sharon Keller online. You were the third, and you were the person he was going to bring disciplinary action against. It would have gotten you thrown out of school, or worse. It would surely have ruined your future career in this field.

"So you killed him, and then you smashed his computer, which you knew had evidence against you. And then, because as his assistant you knew his password, you wrote over the negative evidence in the cloud after he died."

"Rayburn was a piece of garbage," Lusk says. "A drug-addicted piece of garbage."

"He knew what you were, and he died because of it," I say. "I could never understand why Nucci and Borodin would have killed him or smashed his computer. It was against their interests to do so. And it turns out they didn't.

"Anyway, we'll just sit and wait for the police to arrive. I'm sure they will find all they need on your computer and your metaverse headset, which you claimed never to have used.

"Actually, maybe they'll throw the perjury charge in just for fun. Either way, you'll have plenty of time for your law studies."

We wait about twenty minutes more for the police to arrive. I'm actually enjoying watching him squirm. After all, this is a guy who smashed a person over the head with a metal statue.

The cops arrive and place him under arrest, and Marcus and I head back toward Paterson.

Winter is coming to an end; the weather people are saying we won't be getting any more snow.

That means we're heading for a few pleasant weather days before the mosquitoes start arriving. They're probably making travel plans now.

Laurie is already talking with the Rubensteins about taking Ricky and Will back to the Adirondacks during Christmas vacation.

I'm fine with it . . . actually looking forward to it.

I won't be skiing, but I can taste that hot chocolate now.

ABOUT THE AUTHOR

Brandy Allen

David Rosenfelt is the Edgar Award–nominated and Shamus Award–winning author of thirty Andy Carpenter novels, most recently *Dog Day Afternoon*; nine stand-alone thrillers; two nonfiction titles; and four K Team novels, a series featuring some of the characters from the Andy Carpenter series. After years of living in California, he and his wife moved to Maine with twenty-five of the four thousand dogs they have rescued.